FINDING MY SECRET BILLIONAIRE

MY SECRET BILLIONAIRE
BOOK ONE

OLIVIA BHELLE KILDARE

To my family who have always supported me in everything I do and who make everything I do possible.

CONTENTS

CHAPTER ONE

"That's beautiful, Carrie."

Anna Shelby beamed as her student presented her latest artwork assignment. It was only Anna's second year of teaching after graduating from college not long ago, and she loved all the students in her sixth-grade class.

Anna turned twenty-six last month, and since then she had felt like time was getting away from her. She spent hours dreaming about the future she wished she could have, married to a handsome and caring man who adored her, with two children of her own. She wanted a boy and a girl, which she imagined to be the perfect family. In her visions of her perfect future, her children would rush ahead into the shelter they ran for homeless animals, excited to pet the new litter of kittens that had just arrived.

"Do you think it will look good on display in the community center?"

The eager student's voice snapped Anna out of her brief daydream. "Yes, Carrie. I think it will look beautiful on our spring art display."

Anna taught her class at the only school in a small Midwestern town called Belleville, Anna's hometown. The community center was one of only a few larger buildings in the town center, and it was used for most of the events in town, including the school's annual art display. Every class in the school would present their best artwork, so preparing for the unveiling was at the top of Anna's mind for the past several weeks.

Until that afternoon.

Class was over, and Anna went about her routine of putting away supplies and locking up her classroom for the day. She needed to stop by the grocery store on her way home, since she realized that there wasn't anything that wasn't still frozen to make for dinner. Most nights, she ate quietly by herself at home, unless she and her best friend Kelly Skitmore had plans for that night. Kelly also worked at the school as a fifth-grade teacher, and after they both closed up for the afternoon, they passed each other in the hallway.

"I need to grab something at SavingsMart on the way home. Need anything?" Anna asked Kelly.

"No, thanks, John is coming over to make me lasagna," Kelly answered with a huge grin on her face.

"Lucky you! God, I wish I could find the right guy."

"I wish you could, too. I can't wait till we can double date. I hate leaving you alone in that house while I'm having all the fun," said Kelly, her smile falling into a frown.

"It's not that bad," Anna replied. "I spent a lot of time and money fixing up my place. I don't mind spending time there. Besides, I'm so happy for you and John. I think you're perfect together."

Anna wondered when her own luck would change. She'd broken up with her now-ex boyfriend Alan Shangle just a few months before. He was nice at first, but something about the way he treated her just never sat right with Anna. They'd known each other for a long time and had even talked about getting married. She had always dreamed of being treated like a respected princess, but she wondered now if that was just asking too much. Maybe she shouldn't let her dreams interfere with reality, or time really would slip away from her.

"Are you there, Anna? I asked if you had any plans this weekend."

Kelly looked at Anna, concerned, since she seemed to become so distant so quickly.

"Oh, I'm sorry. No. After the art display Friday night, I don't have anything planned, other than I thought I might go shopping in Devon City." Devon City was about an hour away from Belleville. It was a medium-sized city but seemed huge compared with Anna's tiny hometown, with traffic jams and crammed parking lots compared to her town's wide, open spaces. There was only one stoplight in the entire town of Belleville.

"Perfect, I think I'll join you. I need a new dress for the festival next week."

"I'd forgotten about that. I guess I'd better get something for that, too." Anna always had fun at the town's annual festival in the park, which had live music, games, and concession stands with lots of food. Even without a date to accompany her, she had plenty of friends and family members who would attend.

"I'm headed out," Kelly said. "You sure you don't want to join us for dinner?"

"I'm not gonna be a third wheel. You two have a fun night," Anna said, smiling at her best friend.

"Alright, see you tomorrow."

"Bye, Kelly," Anna said, holding her smile until just after Kelly got into her car.

Anna and Kelly had been friends since childhood, which happened often in such a small town. Most people found jobs at the school, at the grocery store, or at a shop on Main Street to try to hold the community together. She'd been happy for Kelly when she finally got together with John, who had also been a friend in school. They hadn't started dating until after college graduation.

Sighing, Anna got in her car and went on her grocery shopping errand.

"Hi, Anna," said the cashier, Elizabeth. Everyone was on a first-name basis in Belleville, and for Elizabeth it was even more casual, since everyone called her Liz.

"Hi, Liz," Anna answered, pulling out a cart and walking on. When she passed by a couple of aisles, she overheard some women whispering and giggling.

"Have you seen that man? Oh, my goodness, he has muscles on top of muscles."

"How could I miss him? It's not like you see that every day here in this town."

"That's for sure. We get Henry at the hardware store, who can barely reach the paint."

The two women laughed more and walked on, not noticing Anna. She giggled to herself and wondered who they were talking about. She hadn't seen anyone handsome and muscle-bound anywhere in Belleville, but she secretly hoped he was shopping on the next aisle.

But that was not the case, and Anna finished her shopping without seeing anyone else in the store. She chose a deli plate for dinner and thought about spending the night catching up on reading.

The giggling women were still gossiping when she got back up to the check-out counter. This time, Liz joined in. Apparently, this mystery man was really something special.

"I would die if that man came up and spoke to me. I'd just die because I wouldn't know what to think or do or say," Liz said excitedly. The other women laughed.

"Who are you all talking about?" Anna asked.

"You haven't seen him? Oh, my goodness, woman, you are missing out. This Greek god of a man came into the store just a few minutes ago. You just missed him. I have no idea who he was, but thank God Regina was at the register then because I would have died." Liz couldn't seem to control herself as the words flew out of her mouth.

"Well, I sure am sorry I missed out on that," laughed Anna. When the women finished their purchase, she paid for her meal and left, driving home.

She pulled into her garage, which was back behind her house. Anna was proud to have bought her own home, and she spent a lot of time decorating the interior and planting flowers in the yard. It was an older home, as were all the houses in the old Midwestern town, but she loved it. She felt so comfortable in it and smiled with pride at being able to purchase a house at her young age.

But she knew there was something missing in her life, and for some reason she felt that more strongly now.

The next day, she found out why.

CHAPTER TWO

THE NEXT DAY WAS THURSDAY, the day before her class was going to present artwork at the school's art display. That morning, Anna decided to leave her daydreams at home and focus on the children, who had worked hard to express their creative ideas. She didn't have children of her own yet, but she could certainly make life enjoyable for the kids in her class, who she loved as if they were her own.

For the most part, she was able to keep her promise to herself, since the day was too hectic to stop and daydream about husbands and children and kittens and animal shelters that didn't exist in her life yet.

One of the other teachers had called in sick, and, as will happen in a small town, there weren't any substitute teachers available to fill in. That meant that Anna, Kelly, and the other teachers all pitched in to help the sick teacher's students get their artwork finished on time. They were all happy to help, and by the end of the day, everyone was ready to head home, including Anna.

This time, she'd remembered to take dinner out of the freezer the night before, so she didn't need to go gossip with Liz at the grocery store again. But she had thought of some things she wanted to do in her yard that weekend, but she needed some gardening supplies. As she started her car to drive home after work, she decided it would be best to get everything that night, since she would be too busy on Friday with the art display.

She headed to the hardware store. It was the only place in town to get gardening supplies, paint, or tools for all the projects Anna had planned for her home, so she went there often. Since it was such a small town, there was much more than hardware on sale there. All the people in the knitting club bought their yarn there, and there were school supplies and even T-shirts and hats with the school's mascot printed on them.

Everything and everyone in the town had to multitask, including the hardware store.

Anna parked her car and headed inside the store, waving at Henry, the store's owner, who was sweeping up near the front door. The cashier, Brent, was talking to someone, but at first Anna didn't look. She just marched ahead to the gardening supplies without a second thought.

But a voice from behind made her heart seem to skip a beat.

"I'm sure glad for your help. It's amazing how friendly people are around here. That's why I moved here." A deep and confident male's voice floated across the room, and when it reached Anna's ears it sounded smooth, soothing, like gentle music.

"You buy a house in town?" asked Brent, the cashier.

"No, I'm out in the country. I'm told it's the old Johnston place. Everyone around here seems to know where everyone lived or even used to live." The man laughed, and the cashier joined in.

Anna walked around to the back of the aisle, afraid to be seen. If this was the handsome stranger that Liz and the ladies spoke about, she definitely didn't want to be the one who embarrassed herself falling over backward when he spoke to her, so she decided to try to get a look at him without him noticing. Luckily, he was busy paying for his purchases, so he wasn't looking around the room.

Liz and the others hadn't exaggerated. He was tall, about six foot three, with a strong, athletic build and beautiful sandy colored hair that flowed gently, as if displaying a softer side of himself. He was wearing jeans and a T-shirt, as most men did in town, but he certainly wore the look better than any other man in Belleville.

He looked up to take the bag from the cashier, and Anna slipped quickly back into the other aisle so she wouldn't be seen. She took a deep breath and was surprised at herself with the way her heart pounded so loudly. She was even afraid he would hear it all the way across the room.

'You're being stupid,' she thought to herself. 'He's just a man. Quit being so rude and shy, Anna,' she chastised herself.

In a small town, friendliness was deeply ingrained in the culture, and Anna had been there all her life. She picked up the flowerpots and other supplies that she'd set down in the other aisle before sneaking a peek at the handsome stranger and walked up toward the counter. Her heart was beating even faster.

The man had just turned around and saw her as he was headed out the door. "Hello," he said politely, in a voice that made her heart melt.

"Hi," Anna managed to say, awe-struck by his gorgeous blue eyes, the exact color of the sky on a clear summer day.

He smiled, seemed to pause for a minute, then walked out the door. Anna was lost in a daydream again, and the cashier cleared his throat to get her attention.

"Oh," she said. "Sorry, here you go, thanks." She placed her flower-pots on the counter, gazing at the door where she'd last seen the man.

Brent laughed lightly. "I swear, every woman in town has the same reaction when they see Ethan Greenfield."

"Ethan?" Anna asked.

"Yeah, that's his name," he said. "He just bought the old Johnston farmhouse on County Road 50 a couple miles out of town. I wish I was as lucky as that guy. I'd have the attention of every woman in Belleville. Of course, the wife might not like it much." He laughed.

Anna giggled, happy to have a release from the awkward tension.

"Thanks," she said, gathering her purchases and heading out the door. By then, Ethan was gone, but he was firmly imprinted in her mind and heart.

She headed home, made herself some dinner, and settled into her daydreams, which now starred Ethan Greenfield. Would he want children? Would he love animals? In her dreams, he certainly did.

She wondered if he knew about the festival next week and hoped she'd see him again there.

CHAPTER THREE

The days passed, and the school's art display had gone well. Anna was thrilled at the way her students excitedly presented their work, and a couple of them even won prizes at the event.

The town's attention turned to the annual festival that would be held over the next weekend in the park. Trucks began arriving all week carrying what would soon be concession booths and small rides for the kids, and tables were set up next to equipment that would soon be used to cook food.

Ever since that day at the hardware store, Anna had thought about Ethan Greenfield. She could barely get her gardening done as she handled the flowerpots and other equipment she'd bought that day, remembering most the way he looked at her with those bright, blue eyes.

With a light workload, Anna's mind had time to wander. She often daydreamed, working out real problems with an imaginary life in her head that made reality easier to manage. She had done it often when she lived with her ex-boyfriend, Alan, who often criticized her. But tonight, her imagination ran wild thinking of Ethan Greenfield and imagining a life with him, with the two kids, the animal shelter, and a happily ever after.

She snapped back into reality after a few minutes, letting the dream fade away.

"He only said hello, Anna," she said aloud to herself. "He didn't sweep you off your feet to the altar. You need to stop with the school-girl crushes. That's what got you in that mess with Alan."

It was late, so she got up, brushed her teeth, and went to bed, with her black fluffy cat, Sammy, curled up at her feet.

* * *

FRIDAY AFTERNOON ARRIVED, AND IT WAS TIME TO HEAD OUT TO THE festival. As with every event in her small Midwestern town, it was a casual celebration, but Anna still wanted to look her best, especially as she wondered whether Ethan Greenfield would be there. She'd put on her favorite sundress that showed off her slender legs and styled her hair in a flowing beach wave look that framed her face to accentuate her features.

Her best friend Kelly was already there when Anna arrived at the park, waving her over from one of the tables near the chili cook-off. Anna smiled and waved back, walking through the crowds of kids running around to be sure they were first in line for the carnival rides.

There was a happy sense of excitement in the air, mixed in with the scent of popcorn and sweet spices from the chili cook-off's crock pots that made Anna realize how hungry she was.

"I'm starving," she said as she plopped down next to Kelly on the picnic table bench.

"Me, too, but I don't think the chili will be ready for a while. I was just thinking about grabbing a cotton candy," Kelly suggested.

"You'll look like a little kid."

"That doesn't bother me!" Kelly exclaimed with a broad smile. "Want one?"

"You know I do," Anna said, laughing.

"Be right back." Kelly walked off toward a nearby concession stand, and Anna took a minute to take in her surroundings.

She couldn't find her parents, but she didn't expect them to be there anyway since they preferred to come to the festival the next morning, when nearby farms brought in their fresh produce to sell.

She was also looking for Ethan Greenfield and was disappointed when she didn't see his muscular figure in the crowd. She hadn't talked about her hardware store encounter with Kelly yet, even though she usually shared everything about her life with her best friend. She didn't want to admit that she was having secret daydreams about an idyllic future with a man she had only seen once, and Kelly could read her thoughts as if they were her own.

Kelly came back soon with the cotton candy and handed Anna a fluffy blue stick of the treat just when Kelly's boyfriend John and some other friends walked toward them.

"None for me?" John joked.

"You're late. No treats for being late," Kelly said to him, then she moved in for a gentle kiss.

"I was helping Randy with his car," John explained. "Hi, Anna. Good to see you."

"Hi, John. I was just keeping your seat warm." Anna laughed as the rest of the group of friends greeted each other.

A while later, she saw him—Ethan Greenfield was walking up to a concession stand halfway across the park from Anna. He looked incredible, in tight jeans that hinted at his muscular frame and a short-sleeved T-shirt that revealed the well-defined muscles of his arms. Anna caught her breath, hoping he would see her and hoping he wouldn't at the same time.

'He only said hello,' she thought, reminding herself that everything she felt about Ethan was just part of a silly daydream. She tried to enjoy the visit with her friends but couldn't shake the nervousness she was feeling.

"Anna, are you alright?" Kelly asked.

"I'm fine. It's just a little hot out here," Anna replied. "Maybe I'll go get a drink."

"I can get you one," John offered.

"No, thank you. I think I need to walk around a bit anyway." Anna felt like she needed to get away from the friendly but prying eyes of Kelly before she started reading her mind.

"Okay, don't be long, girl!" Kelly said with a smile before she turned back to the conversation at the table.

Anna got up and walked across the park, the opposite way from where she'd seen Ethan. She kept telling herself that he would never remember her, anyway. A man like that would have plenty of girlfriends around.

As she walked up to a concession stand offering cool drinks, a smooth, confident voice surprised her from behind.

"Hello. I think we met in the hardware store the other day?"

Anna turned around and there he stood, Ethan Greenfield in all his muscular glory. Her heart leaped a bit in her chest.

"Hi. Um, yes, I think we did," Anna managed to say. "I'm Anna. Anna Shelby."

"Hello, Anna Shelby. Can I buy you a drink?" said Ethan.

"Sure," she answered in a voice that almost squeaked. She felt the warm flow of blood flushing her face. "I was just getting an orange soda."

"Two orange sodas, please," Ethan told the cashier, who scooped up ice into two paper cups and filled them with the colorful drink. Ethan gave the cashier money and handed one of the drinks to Anna. "Keep the change."

"Thank you, sir," the young cashier said, smiling broadly.

Ethan turned to Anna. "I just moved into the old Johnston's place on Road 50. I'm new to Belleville, but everyone's been really nice. I'm assuming you're a local?"

"Yes, I was born and raised here," she explained, suddenly wondering if she had blue lips from the cotton candy. It was too late to pull out a mirror. "I teach sixth grade at the school."

"That's wonderful. The teachers of the world really do shape our future." He smiled at her, meeting her gaze with those amazing sky-blue eyes.

"Thanks," Anna replied. "I try to do my best. Oh, and thanks for the drink," she added.

"You're quite welcome. I'm really looking forward to that chili contest." Ethan said.

"Yes, it's always delicious. It's quite an important competition around here." Anna explained.

They continued for a while with polite small talk, looking into each other's eyes. Anna was nervous, and with every statement, she felt like kicking herself for not saying something more meaningful.

As they spoke, neither Anna nor Ethan noticed the man standing off in the distance with short brown hair, his green eyes squinting in the sun and a bitter look of contempt on his face.

"I'd better get back to my friends before they worry," Anna said after a few minutes. She didn't think she could stand there for a second longer without doing something embarrassing like tripping over herself or, worse, spilling her drink all over Ethan. It was better to just cut the conversation short for now.

"Of course. Yes, I wouldn't want them to worry. I'll see you around more, I'm sure." Ethan looked gently into Anna's emerald green eyes.

"Yes, yes. I'll–I'll be here all weekend." She instantly regretted how desperate she sounded. "And thank you again for the drink."

"It was my pleasure," he said, and Anna smiled and walked away, feeling her heart pounding in her chest.

Heading back to the picnic table, she noticed a familiar look on Kelly's face. 'Oh, no, they all saw that,' she thought in a panic.

"Sooo," said Kelly, drawing out the word. "That looked--interesting." She giggled.

"Don't you start. I was just being polite. He's new in town." Anna flashed a furrowed-brow look at her friend that told her to let the subject drop.

"Okay, okay. Yep, folks, let's move on, nothing to see here," Kelly joked.

The whole table laughed as Anna's face turned beat red, and she slipped into a seat next to Kelly.

"I'm gonna get you for this," she whispered, and Kelly smiled.

CHAPTER FOUR

THE WEEKEND HAD BEEN EXHAUSTING for Anna, who normally found the festival to be a much-needed time to relax. Instead, this year she'd been constantly nervous, looking around for Ethan and dodging all the teasing comments from friends. Kelly had backed off as the weekend went on, and Anna knew she'd get an earful later when there was no one else around.

Anna had run into Ethan more than once, and it almost seemed like he was looking for her as much as she was looking for him.

'That was all just my imagination,' she thought. 'Of course he would be at a major festival in a new town. He's just trying to meet people.'

The excitement of the weekend hadn't calmed down for the students in her classroom, so Anna was too busy all day to do much daydreaming, and she was grateful. She managed to get her class back into learning mode for the rest of the day, then she spent all afternoon planning lessons for the rest of the week.

"What a day!" Kelly said as she popped her head into the classroom, noticing Anna busy with her papers. "You're still doing plans?"

"Yes, almost done though," Anna answered.

"Dinner tonight?" Kelly asked.

"I'm so exhausted. I have some leftovers of stuff I bought at the festival that I think I'll just heat up, then I'm gonna pass out early," Anna replied.

"Okay. Yeah, I'm tired too. But are you sure there's nothing you want to chat about?" As usual, Kelly was very good at reading her friend's mind.

"There is, but I just don't have the energy tonight. Tomorrow?"

"It's a date," Kelly agreed. "John has to work late all this week, so we'll get together for some girl talk."

"Sounds good. I'll see you tomorrow," Anna called out as Kelly turned to leave.

"See you, girl!"

Alone, Anna sighed and looked out at her empty classroom for a few minutes before she went back to finishing up her work. Finally, she put away her papers, locked the door, and headed out to her car.

Once home, she was happy to be there, and she looked forward to the leftover chili and cornbread waiting for her in her fridge. 'An easy dinner, and a good one, too,' she thought, pulling out the Styrofoam packages and arranging it in a bowl for the microwave. Sammy looked up at her and meowed, and she picked him up to pet him.

"You're not getting this chili, young man. It won first prize!" Suddenly, her doorbell rang. "Well, who could that be ruining my dinner?" Anna asked herself.

Standing on her porch was a skinny young delivery boy holding an oversized vase of red roses. "Flower delivery, ma'am."

"For me?" Anna asked.

"Yes, Miss Shelby," the boy said. Every young person in town knew the woman who taught sixth grade at their school.

"Thank you," Anna said, reaching into her pocket to hand the boy a couple of dollar bills.

"Thanks," the boy said, handing her the flowers and turning away.

As she walked back inside, instantly she thought of Ethan.

'But how would he know where I lived?' she thought, instantly answering her own question in her mind, since he could have asked anyone in town for her address.

She opened the card and nearly squealed with delight, thrilled that she was by herself so that she didn't have to hold back her excitement. Sammy looked up at her. "Well, I don't have to hide my feelings around you at least," she said aloud.

The flowers really were from Ethan Greenfield. 'Thanks for sharing a drink. I'd love to get together for dinner so we can talk more. My number is 555-5656. Please give me a call. Ethan Greenfield.'

Anna was thrilled that he wanted to go out, but something inside her made her pause. She'd had a rough breakup from her ex-boyfriend Alan, and she was just starting to get to the point where she could go about her day without bad memories. The invitation brought them back to the surface, and she sank into a chair as those memories poured into her mind.

"I don't know why you think you could do something like that," Alan had once told her. "That takes a lot of planning and organization and you can't get that done. You're completely disorganized. Everything is a mess here in this house. It's not just petting kittens, you know. It's a business, and you need brains to run a business. You need to think things through before you start having crazy ideas, Anna." Alan had said that to her after she had opened up about her dream of running a shelter for homeless animals. It was just one of the many times where he had insisted that she wasn't good enough or smart enough to do something, and over time, Anna started to believe it.

Eventually, she gave up pursuing any idea that Alan said was crazy and relaxed into a comfortable life teaching school in her tiny hometown. It wasn't that she didn't want to teach. She loved her students and felt like her job was meaningful. She just wanted to add to her life, supplementing it with more things that would make her feel happy and useful. Alan never understood.

It took a couple of years for Anna to finally get up the courage to break it off with Alan. Their relationship had gone through many stages, and at one point, she had been convinced that she should marry him so she could finally have the family she wanted. Time was passing quickly, after all.

But something about Anna accepting his proposal emboldened Alan, and his personality seemed to deteriorate. He started wanting to make all the decisions, always calling Anna crazy for any idea she would tell him about.

She finally stopped telling him anything, and soon she felt like a robot, blindly obeying Alan's commands. In the end, Kelly convinced her that it was no way to spend the rest of her life and helped her finally break it off with Alan.

As all these memories flooded back into her mind, tears ran down her cheeks. How could she ever go through all that again? Starting a new relationship could end in just as much heartache if not more, and Anna didn't know if she had the strength.

"Kelly. I've got to talk to Kelly," she said aloud to Sammy, who purred softly in her lap.

CHAPTER FIVE

"Finally, we get a fun evening together," Kelly said as Anna walked into Kelly and John's small and tastefully decorated home.

Anna and Kelly had been inseparable friends since childhood, going to the same school together and both teaching at that same school, but for the past few years, Anna's complicated relationship with Alan had given Anna and Kelly less leisure time together.

Anna's engagement to Alan Shangle had been a difficult time for their friendship as Alan made more and more demands on Anna's time. Kelly always suspected that Alan did that just to keep Anna isolated, away from the positive influence of Kelly's friendship.

After the breakup, Anna and Kelly spent more time together, but as Kelly's relationship bloomed with John, Anna always wanted to be sure to leave space for that relationship to develop. She knew John and Kelly were the perfect match.

"I'm so happy," said Anna as she sat down in her friend's living room, "and I have so much to talk over with you."

"Oh, that sounds like a handsome-new-man-is-in-town-and-I-want-him sort of talk, and I can't wait!" Kelly brushed her long, straight blonde hair away from her face. "But first, we need some girl's night snack food. I can't talk about men on an empty stomach."

Anna laughed. "I agree. Let's get a few snacks first. I require salt and sugar immediately."

Both friends laughed together as they headed toward the kitchen. Anna started rummaging through Kelly's cupboards as if they were her own as Kelly pulled out some dishes. Eventually, they had bowls of pretzels, potato chips, and candy-coated chocolates arranged in bowls on Kelly's kitchen table, where they both sat down.

"Well, not exactly health food, but who cares? It's our night to have fun," said Kelly.

"Remember that dinner party we planned when you first moved here? This reminds me of that. The menu sounded like heaven for a kids' sleepover." Both friends giggled at the memory.

A few years ago, they'd hosted their first adults-only party. They had both planned it for months but realized only a couple days before the event that the menu of pizza, hot dogs, chips, and cookies sounded like something kids would make raiding the fridge when their parents weren't home. Anna and Kelly laughed as they reminisced about the party and some of the other good times they'd spent together.

"Oh, and I talked to Bree the other day," Anna said.

"I haven't seen her since college. How is she doing?"

"Pretty good," Anna explained. "She's still in the city."

"I'll have to give her a call. But stop stalling," Kelly said. "Let's get to the dirt on you and Mister Gorgeous."

"I'm not stalling. I was getting there," Anna said with a laugh.

"Mmm hmm, sure." Kelly smiled.

"Anyway, there's no dirt. Zero dirt. But he asked me out."

"Oh, my goodness! Well, that would be dirt, my friend," Kelly said with a laugh. "What did he say? How did he say it? Tell me before I die of curiosity!"

"He didn't say anything. He sent flowers with a card."

"Flowers! Oh, my goodness. That's so romantic." Kelly smiled broadly, obviously happy for her friend.

"Red roses."

"Wow, big spender. Even better." They both laughed.

"He gave me his number," Anna added.

"So, what did he say when you called him?"

"Nothing, I haven't called."

Kelly almost dropped the pretzel she had just grabbed from the bowl. "What? Why not?"

"I don't know if I'm ready," Anna replied.

"Ready. Ready? Oh, my greatest friend of all friends, how is it that you're not ready to date a gorgeous man who sends red roses? Did I mention that he's gorgeous?" Kelly plopped the pretzel into her mouth.

"Well, gorgeous isn't the only thing in the world."

"Yes, yes. He's also a big spender," Kelly teased.

Anna laughed. "And money isn't all there is in life, either. I just don't want to go jumping into something like a crazed schoolgirl just because a handsome, muscular man asks me out."

"Oh, those muscles," Kelly said, turning her blue eyes up and plopping her chin on her hand. "I mean, I love John and he looks great, but oh, the muscles on your guy. Damn, that man is built."

"Well yeah, of course I did notice that, but still," Anna said, shaking herself before she started on another daydream about Ethan's good looks. "I need to know I'm not going to get hurt."

"My dear Anna, you know I love you," Kelly began, her demeanor turning serious. "I'm your best friend in the world, and I don't ever want to see you hurt. But if you don't take a risk and take a chance, you'll hurt in the end because you missed out on something in your life. I want the best for you, so I want you to take this chance. You need to call this man right away."

"You're right. I'm just scared." Anna plopped a candy into her mouth.

"You've been daydreaming about him, haven't you?" Kelly asked.

"Ugh, you have to stop reading my mind. You know that's scary, right?" Anna said, forcing a smile so her friend wouldn't worry.

"Too bad," Kelly said. "We're forever joined in the mind. Once you're daydreaming, I know you're serious about a guy. And I know you've also been sitting in your house stewing about all that wasted time with Alan, too."

"I wouldn't trade our friendship for anything. You're right. I've been thinking about Alan, and I don't want a repeat of that disaster."

"Neither do I," Kelly said. "But I've seen this new man around town, and he seems so nice with everyone. I just have this feeling that he's different, that he's right for you. I really want you to give him a chance." She paused. "I don't even know his name. What's his name?"

"Ethan Greenfield."

"Ethan Greenfield," Kelly repeated in a dreamy voice. "Well, this Ethan Greenfield is about to get a phone call. Do you have his number on you?"

"Yes, I put it in my phone. I just haven't had the guts to call him yet," Anna replied.

"Well, you'll get no more snacks from me," Kelly said, pulling back the chocolate dish, "until you get on that phone and call that beautiful man."

"Stop that. Okay, fine, you win." Anna laughed. She paused for a few minutes to think of what she would say to Ethan. Then she took her cellphone out of her purse, found her new contact, and clicked on it, closing her eyes as the phone rang on the other end.

CHAPTER SIX

"Hello?" Anna thought Ethan's voice sounded even more sexy and soothing over the phone.

"Hi, is this Ethan? This is Anna, Anna Shelby," Anna said, her voice a bit shaky.

"Well, hello there, Anna Shelby. I'm so glad you called," he answered.

"I got your roses. They were very beautiful, thank you."

"Only half as beautiful as you, and it's my pleasure," Ethan replied. Anna blushed, happy that the conversation wasn't in person. "Have you given any thought to my invitation?"

"Yes," Anna answered. "I'd love to join you for dinner."

"Wonderful, where would you like to go?"

"Well, I know this nice Italian place in Chesterville called Tony's. Do you know where that is?" Anna asked.

"I can find it. It's pretty easy to find everything in the little towns around here. How about this Saturday? Can I pick you up around seven?"

Anna felt a rush of fear. Was she really going on a date with this gorgeous stranger? She didn't really know anything about him. "I need to go to Chesterville Saturday anyway, so I can meet you there at Tony's at seven."

Kelly lifted her eyebrows, but Anna waved her off with her free hand.

"That sounds perfect, Anna. I'm looking forward to it. I'll see you then," Ethan answered.

"I'll see you then. Bye-bye," Anna said nervously.

"Goodbye."

Anna put her phone away. "Don't look at me like that, Kelly. This guy could be a stalker or a serial killer for all I know. I'm not getting in a car with him yet."

"I know," Kelly said, laughing. "I'm just giving you a hard time."

Anna and Kelly spent the rest of the night watching old movies, munching on snacks, and talking about good times, but in the back of her mind, Anna couldn't stop thinking about the date.

* * *

Saturday came quickly, and Anna was ready for her date. She had changed her mind about what to wear a dozen times and finally settled on a floral dress that showed off her curves but wasn't too formal. The restaurants in all the towns around her home were very casual.

When she arrived at Tony's Italian Cuisine, she realized that she didn't even know what kind of car Ethan drove. Seeing no one in the parking lot, she gave her lipstick a final check in her rearview mirror and double-checked the charge on her cellphone before throwing it in her purse. Kelly and Anna had devised a plan in case Anna felt unsafe on her date, so being able to text her from the ladies' room was a must.

She walked into the restaurant and didn't see anyone waiting nearby.

"Good evening, ma'am. Do you have a reservation?" The energetic young hostess greeted her with a smile.

"Oh," Anna answered, having not even considered that she needed a reservation. "It might be under Greenfield, for two."

"Yes, I see it here. Mr. Greenfield is already here. I'll show you to your table."

"Thanks," Anna said, surprised that Ethan had arrived early.

The hostess weaved her through a few rows of tables to a booth way in the back. It was quiet there, and the soft lighting gave off a warm, flickering glow like a candle.

"Hello, Anna," Ethan said, rising from his chair to greet her.

"I hope you didn't wait long," she answered timidly. She had been hoping all day for a quiet table where no one from Belleville might see her on her date so she wouldn't have to deal with gossip. But the reality of being alone with Ethan in such a romantic setting suddenly made her nervous.

"No, not long at all. This is a nice restaurant, nice people. I was just looking over the menu." Ethan answered.

The hostess handed her a menu. "Can I get you a drink to start?" she asked.

"I'll have an iced tea, no sugar, please," Anna said.

"I'll be right back," the hostess said with a smile.

Alone with Ethan for the first time, Anna stared at her menu but couldn't concentrate. 'Don't do anything stupid, Anna,' she thought to herself. 'Just order the lasagna plate again. It was good last time.'

She looked at Ethan with a nervous smile. He seemed so calm and confident, the opposite of what she was feeling at that moment. He wore a loose-fitting button-up shirt that matched his blue eyes with the top button undone. It was the perfect look for the restaurant's atmosphere. Anna noticed his well-defined arm muscles but tried not to stare.

"The hostess recommends the lasagna, so I think I'll give that a try. Do you need more time with the menu?" he asked.

"No, that sounds delicious. I think I'll try it, too," Anna answered.

A waitress appeared and took their order, then left them alone in the flickering warm light once again.

"I'm getting a lot of renovations done on my farmhouse. I'm really excited about being here out in the country. It seems like such an idyllic lifestyle." Ethan said, breaking the silence.

"Where are you from?" Anna asked.

"Los Angeles. Needless to say, it's a huge difference out here in the Midwestern farmlands."

"Wow, yes, that's quite a difference. You won't have to worry about traffic at all." She laughed.

He smiled. "That's one thing I'll never miss. I really love it here."

"I'm glad," Anna said. "I just don't think I'd be comfortable anywhere else."

They talked between ordering their meals and waiting for the food. She felt the nervousness melt away as she got to know Ethan more. He seemed perfectly in tune with her, gently steering the conversation at first but then giving her the space to bring up subjects she wanted to talk about as she grew more comfortable. They spoke about her job, her friends, and her family, as well as Ethan's family and the farmhouse he was renovating.

"So, what do you see in your future?" he asked.

"This will sound silly, but I've always wanted to open an animal shelter," she explained. "I've loved pets all my life and have always felt sorry for those that didn't have a home. I want to someday make a difference for those animals that need me."

"That's amazing," Ethan said. "I've always had a dog or cat, or both, in my life, and I can't imagine a home without a pet. Right now, I have Teddy and Milo. Teddy's a German shepherd with an attitude, but he also loves to snuggle like a teddy bear. Milo is a crazy tabby cat who thinks he's the boss of Teddy."

Anna laughed, happy that Ethan had a soft spot in his heart for animals just like her.

"Since I've been here, I've added a few rescue farm animals as well," he added.

"I just have Sammy right now. He's a black, fluffy cat who also thinks he's in charge."

"Well, then, they should all get along great," Ethan said, smiling.

The more they talked, the more they found they had in common, and as the dinner date went on, Anna felt like she could tell Ethan anything. There wouldn't be a need to text Kelly on this night, and she smiled at the thought of her friend being happy about that.

The lasagna arrived and it was delicious as expected, and they both ordered coffee, since there was a bit of a drive home and neither wanted a cocktail.

"Do you want dessert?" Ethan asked.

"I'd love some, but I don't think I have room," Anna replied. "Maybe I'll just stick with the coffee."

"I agree. That lasagna was amazing, but filling," he said.

Time flew by as they continued to talk, and slowly the tables around them started to empty. "These nice people probably want to close up," he said after a while.

"I don't want to leave," she said.

"Neither do I," he said as his blue eyes gazed into hers. "But we don't want anyone getting mad at us."

They both chuckled and rose from the table, and Ethan paid the bill on the way out. Anna noticed that he left a large tip.

Anna and Ethan walked slowly through the parking lot, as if slowing down would somehow keep the night from ever ending. As they reached Anna's car, Ethan took her hand.

"I had a wonderful night," he said.

"So did I," she agreed.

"Let's do this again. This time I pick the restaurant, and we'll see if I can choose as well as you."

"Okay." She laughed. "How about next weekend?"

"Friday?" he asked.

"Yes, that's perfect," she said.

They paused, his warm hand still nestled hers as they gazed at each other. Anna thought about kissing him, but she wanted him to make the first move. He started to move in slightly but seemed to be stopping himself.

"Goodnight, Anna," he said.

"Goodnight, Ethan. I'll see you Friday." Anna's hand reluctantly slid off his as she got into her car, and he closed the door. They waved once more at each other, and Ethan walked away. Anna sighed, put on her seatbelt, and started her car for the ride home.

CHAPTER SEVEN

ALMOST A WEEK HAD PASSED, and Anna and Ethan had been talking on the phone almost every day. Anna was happy, but nervous at the same time because she was afraid her relationship with Ethan was just too good to be true.

Kelly disagreed strongly, nearly squealing with delight when Anna had told her how the first date had gone.

"This is right for you, I know it. I feel it," Kelly had told Anna.

It was Friday, and Anna had been excited all day about the second date. Ethan had chosen a restaurant in Bluewater, a larger city about an hour's drive away from Belleville.

It was almost time for Ethan to pick her up, and Anna was putting some finishing touches on her makeup. Ethan had chosen a more formal restaurant in the city, so she had gone shopping with Kelly earlier in the week and bought a deep green dress that formed perfectly to her figure and matched the color of her emerald eyes. Green was always a perfect color for her, not only because of her eye color, but also because it accentuated the color in her reddish-brown hair, which for her date that night she had styled into a messy updo with accessories that matched her dress.

"You look incredible," Ethan said as she greeted him at the door.

"Thanks. You look pretty awesome yourself," she told him. She had never seen him in formal wear before, and she swore the dark grey suit he wore looked perfectly tailored to fit him. For a minute, she wondered about that, since no man in Belleville had ever worn a tailored suit. She dismissed the thought, assuming that he had just found the perfect size.

As they walked out to her driveway, she was surprised to see a car with a driver waiting for them.

"Oh, you hired a driver," Anna said.

"It's a long drive, and I thought we might want to get cocktails before the performance."

"Performance?" she asked, surprised.

"I got us tickets to the theater. I hope you don't mind. I read that tonight's performance is a pretty popular play," Ethan explained.

"Wow, dinner and a show. This will be fun!" Anna exclaimed.

They climbed into the back seat and the driver headed to Bluewater. Along the way, they passed acres of farmland, with rolling hills divided into fields of crops that blanketed the landscape in different shades of green.

"Well, this certainly isn't LA," Ethan joked.

"I've never been there. What's it like?" Anna asked.

"Crowded. Smoggy. But it definitely has a few good points," he said.

"You'll have to show me someday."

"It's a date," he answered, smiling.

When they arrived in Bluewater, dinner was first on the night's agenda, and the driver pulled up in front of The Trinity Oceana, a well-known, high-end restaurant specializing in European cuisine.

* * *

THE FOOD WAS EVERYTHING THE CRITICS HAD RAVED ABOUT IN THE restaurant's online reviews, and Anna and Ethan enjoyed some after-dinner drinks as they talked more about everything they had in common.

"What's your work like?" she asked.

"I actually work from home most of the time. I do a little investing and property management," he explained.

"You must be very good at it. It sounds exciting," Anna said.

"I do okay. It's a living," he added, smiling.

With the play about to start, Anna and Ethan left the restaurant to head for the theater. Anna was surprised that the same driver and car appeared again to pick them up. She had assumed Ethan had rented a car service so different cars in the same service would drive them at different times.

"You rented it for the whole night?" she asked. "That must have been expensive."

"It was nothing," he said, giving a quick sideways look to the driver that Anna didn't notice. Once in the car, they left for the theater.

* * *

ANNA LOVED THE PLAY AND WAS SURPRISED THAT ETHAN SEEMED TO enjoy it as well. "Not many men appreciate the theater," she told him as they walked out of the theater.

"It fascinates me as an art form. I find live theater more interesting than watching movies, which are mostly just computerized effects," he explained.

"I agree," she smiled as they stepped into the car. It was late, and since the drive home was long, they both agreed that they would leave the city and head back to Belleville.

* * *

ARRIVING AT HER HOUSE, THEY LAUGHED AS HE WALKED HER TO THE door. Anna was trying to stay quiet to keep the neighbors from hearing them and coming out to look. She didn't like being a source of gossip in the small town, and she knew everyone would talk about her dating the new, handsome man in town.

"That driver must be so bored having to wait for us all night," she observed.

"I'm sure he brought things along to do while we had fun. And I had a lot of fun tonight, Anna," Ethan said, gazing into her eyes. "You look incredible," he added.

She smiled. "I had a wonderful time, too," she agreed.

They were both feeling the effects of the night's cocktails. They hadn't had many, but it was enough to relax. He moved in closer to Anna, never releasing his gaze from her emerald eyes. She felt drawn to him. Soon they were so close that they both knew what would happen next. His lips met hers as she relaxed into his kiss, parting her lips as an invitation for a deeper embrace. She felt the warmth of his hands on her back as he held her tightly, as if he never wanted to let her go. After a few minutes, they parted reluctantly, and as they did so, their fingers slid down each other's arms until they were holding hands. He squeezed both her hands gently.

"Goodnight, Anna. I can't wait for our next time together," he said.

"We'll do it soon," she answered.

"Next weekend, I'd like to show you my place."

"That sounds great. I can't wait," Anna answered with a dreamy smile. He gave her hand one last squeeze before they parted, and she went inside her house.

* * *

"Hmm," said the driver as Ethan got back into the car, "that was--interesting," he laughed.

"Don't start with me, Rick," Ethan laughed, then relaxed into the seat. "But seriously, thanks so much for taking us. I don't think it would have worked out trying to drive ourselves, but I didn't want to be obvious with the limo."

"I don't think she knows," Rick said as he started driving Ethan home, "but it's something you need to tell her very soon."

"I know," answered Ethan. "She's coming out to the house next weekend."

"And you're showing her everything?" asked Rick.

"I'm not sure."

"Ethan, you're my best friend, and you need to listen to me on this one. I've never seen you like this before, so don't let this one get away," Rick said in a concerned voice, glaring at Ethan in his rearview mirror as he drove.

"I know, I won't. I'm not sure yet when to tell her. But there's one thing I'm sure of."

"What's that?" Rick asked.

"I'm falling in love with Anna Shelby," Ethan answered.

CHAPTER EIGHT

Anna slept soundly the night of the date, although she had expected to lay awake daydreaming with excitement. Maybe it was the alcohol. Or maybe it was contentment, that feeling she always hoped for that would tell her she no longer had to daydream about the perfect life.

A few days passed, and Anna and Kelly paused for a few minutes in the parking lot after work to have a chat.

"I'm almost as excited about next weekend as you are," laughed Kelly.

"I'm thrilled, but I'm also a little uncertain," Anna told her friend.

"Uncertain? Girl, you need to stop letting those demons of your past mess with your future. Please, try to forget about that stupid Alan," Kelly begged.

"I'm trying. Believe me, I'm trying," Anna answered. "I'm headed for the grocery store. Need anything for dinner?"

"Okay fine, change the subject," Kelly teased. "I do, but I need to run home first to grab my shopping list, so I'll be right behind you."

"Okay, I'll see you there," said Anna.

Both women drove off for their respective errands, and soon Anna pulled into the grocery store parking lot. She rummaged through her purse before going in to find her own shopping list. Finally, she located it and got out of her car.

A familiar voice made her stop in her tracks.

"What do you think you're doing, fooling around with that guy?" Alan Shangle approached her hollering and quickly moved right up into her face.

Shocked, Anna took a second to compose herself, but thankfully she was able to respond. When she and Alan first broke up, Kelly had helped her practice being more assertive so Alan would stop being so possessive of her and hopefully stop bothering her.

"It's not any concern of yours what I do," said Anna. Her voice sounded confident from all the practice, but she felt every part of her body shaking. That old, familiar fear reappeared quickly.

"Oh, it isn't, is it? Well, I guess Little Miss Anna thinks she knows how the world works, doesn't she? You always were an idiot. No guy like that is gonna want you for anything but s-e-x," he said, spelling out the word for emphasis.

"That's not true," was all Anna could think of to say.

"Whatever. You're a liar, and everyone knows it. That guy'll figure it out soon enough. You promised to be my wife, and we saw how that went. You're still gonna marry me one day. You just don't know it yet," Alan said with a sour look on his face.

"I'm not a liar. I have a right to change my mind about important things like who I'm going to marry," Anna answered. Her nerves were rattled, but she pictured Kelly supporting her in every word she said.

"You'll see. You'll be seeing a lot more of me real soon, and a lot less of Mr. Muscles," said Alan.

"Alan Shangle, if you don't get your grimy paws away from her, you'll answer to me!" Kelly had arrived and saw Alan harassing Anna. She'd barely shut down her car before she bounded out to confront the man.

"Oh, your bodyguard is here, I see," teased Alan with malice in his voice, looking over Kelly, his eyes lingering on her chest long enough to be sure she noticed.

"Leave, you disgusting pig," Kelly commanded, and Alan started to back away. He had always been afraid of her boyfriend, John, who was stronger and smarter than Alan.

"Remember me in your dreams, dear," he called out to Anna as he left.

"Ugh, that man is repulsive," Kelly said as she turned to Anna. "Are you alright?"

"Yes, thanks, I think so," said Anna, "I think I did okay with him. He said I'd see a lot more of him. I hope he's not planning something."

"He's too chicken and stupid to plan anything, Anna," Kelly reassured her. "Try not to worry about him."

"I'll try," Anna said, adjusting her dress. "Let's just go shopping."

"You've got it!" Kelly answered.

The women did their shopping, and Anna was thankful that Alan was still gone after she was done.

"Keep your phone out handy," Kelly told her. "If he comes around your house, text or call me pronto!"

"I will. Thanks, hun," Anna said, giving her friend a goodbye hug.

Anna arrived home and was happy again that there was no sign of Alan in her neighborhood. He lived across town, so most of the time he was normally easy to avoid. She hadn't seen much of him at all until her dates with Ethan.

"He must be watching me," she said to herself as she plopped down her things on her kitchen table and picked up Sammy for a hug. "He's going to stay away from us, Sammy. Don't you worry about Alan Shangle." But it wasn't her cat who was worried.

It was hard for Anna to eat dinner that night. Something bothered her in the pit of her stomach. Her relationship with Alan had gone badly, but it wasn't always like that. She recalled some of their first dates like they were yesterday. At first, Alan had been so kind and polite, seemingly listening to her every word and agreeing with almost every decision she made.

"When did that change?" she asked aloud to herself, "And why?" The memories flooded into her mind, and there seemed to be as many good times as bad times. 'Maybe it was all my fault after all,' she thought.

Then her thoughts turned to Ethan and the wonderful conversations they shared. 'Is it all just the same?' she wondered. 'Maybe he's not being genuine, either, and he's just impressing me and really doesn't care about me or animals or anything he claims we have in common at all. Kelly likes him, but she's never even met him, so she really doesn't know him. I just don't think I can go through that kind of mess again.'

She reached down to pet Sammy, who was now nestled in a ball, purring in her lap. "I can't do it again, Sammy. I don't have the strength."

She sat for a moment. 'I need to tell Ethan that I'm just not ready,' she thought. 'This will be hard. But going through all that again would be harder.' She pulled out her phone and pulled up Ethan's number in her contacts.

She stared at the phone for several minutes, then clicked on the button to call him.

CHAPTER NINE

"ANNA, hello. I was just thinking about you," said Ethan when he picked up his phone.

"Hi Ethan. I've been thinking about you, too," Anna answered in a shaky voice.

"What's wrong? I sense a 'but' coming next in that sentence," Ethan said, concerned.

"Well, it's not anything I want to talk about over the phone. Can you meet me for dinner tomorrow at Tony's? I think we need to talk."

"Yes, of course," Ethan answered reluctantly. He sensed there was something very wrong in Anna's voice. "Will around seven work for you? Or I could pick you up earlier ..."

"Seven will work, thanks. I'll just meet you there again, if that's okay," answered Anna.

"Yes, that's fine. I guess I'll see you then."

"See you then. Take care, bye Ethan," Anna said, quickly hanging up the call. She winced and let out a deep breath, knowing she had worried him and most likely hurt his feelings. This was going to be hard. She'd have to stay strong.

She looked down at Sammy, still sitting contently in her lap.

"You're so lucky, nothing in life is hard for you," she said aloud as a tear fell from her eye.

* * *

ANNA PULLED INTO THE PARKING LOT OF TONY'S ITALIAN CUISINE feeling nervous again, but it wasn't the same feeling as she'd had when she had arrived at that same restaurant for her first date with Ethan. This time, she felt a sense of dread at having to break off the relationship. She remained convinced that Ethan wasn't really interested in her the way she had originally thought, and constantly reminding herself of that gave her a twinge of courage to go through with it.

This time she had made the reservations herself and arrived early so she could be there before him. She didn't want to sit at the romantic, dimly lit booth in the back. Instead, she'd reserved a table near the front that would feel more like a business meeting.

"Anna, hello. You look lovely, as always," Ethan greeted her as the hostess brought him to the table.

"Hi, you look great, too. You always look great." She tried to smile politely but couldn't manage much of a smile.

Ethan sat down at the table and the hostess left.

"Well, this certainly feels different from our other dates," Ethan observed. "What is it you need to talk about?"

"It's us. Well, there's not really an us, but I just need to stop this almost an us business before there is an us," Anna blurted out, barely understanding what she had just said herself.

"Okay," Ethan said, slowly elongating the word. "What's brought this on? Is it something I said or did?"

"No. No, it's not you. It's me. I just can't do this again," she said, fighting back tears.

Ethan looked confused, but he fought to regain his composure, his face shifting into a look of concern. "Anna, what is it? What has happened that changed what we were building together? What is it that you can't do again?" he asked.

"I... I just can't go through the pain again. It's all starting again, and I just don't have the strength for it." Anna realized that it sounded like she was babbling, but she couldn't find the words to explain how she felt. "I just need some time. I'm not ready."

"Anna, I could never rush you into anything you're not ready for. If this all feels too sudden for you, I understand. Let's slow down a bit so you're more comfortable," said Ethan. He wanted to be understanding with her, but he really couldn't understand why she had changed so suddenly.

"Are we ready to order?" asked the young waitress as she walked up to the table. She instantly noticed the tension and nearly walked backward away from the table. "I'm sorry, I can come back," she said, starting to walk away.

"No, that's fine," Ethan said, calling her back. "Can you get us a couple of lasagna plates to go, please?" He remembered how much she enjoyed the dish on their first date.

"Yeah, sure," the waitress said, then hurried away.

"I really don't think I could eat a bite," said Anna, fighting back tears.

"You'll be hungry later. I just want to be sure you have something," Ethan explained.

"Thank you," said Anna. "I know it's hard to understand. I can't even explain it. I just need more time right now, that's all," she added.

"It's okay, Anna," he answered. "We have all the time in the world."

"I'm sorry," she said.

"There's nothing to be sorry about, Anna," said Ethan.

When the waitress returned with the meals packaged to go, Ethan paid the check and they left the restaurant. He walked her to her car.

"I'm sorry," she said once again.

"Don't be, Anna. We're just slowing things down a bit to make you comfortable. Are you okay to drive? I could take you …"

"I'm fine," she answered, cutting him off. "I'm okay."

She got into her car and gave him half a wave. She couldn't bear to look at him anymore with all the tears running down her face. She started the car and drove away, leaving him standing in the parking lot. He paused for a few minutes trying to figure out what had happened, then drove himself home.

* * *

"I don't get it, either, Ethan," Rick said later that night as they sat out on deck outside his farmhouse, each with a glass of scotch. "But I'll tell you one thing. You ARE hiding something from her. She's a smart woman, and she can sense that. Who knows what she's imagining? In her head, you could be a serial killer or something. I'm telling you, keeping this from her is keeping you both apart."

"You're right. But now how do I tell her? She needs some time, and all I can do is give it to her. I can't just blurt out everything about all this," he said, waving his arms around to indicate the farmland as he emphasized the word, "if she doesn't want to see me right now."

"Oh, that woman wants to see you, my friend," Rick repeated. "She wants to see you."

"Maybe, but I'm going to give her a couple of days. She has to work anyway, so I'll give her some time to think, and then I'll talk to her on the weekend," Ethan said, staring up at the stars and taking a sip of his scotch.

CHAPTER TEN

A FEW DAYS HAD PASSED, and Anna still felt uneasy about breaking it off with Ethan. She'd been distracted every day at work and felt like she wasn't giving her students her all because she just couldn't focus. Kelly had noticed a difference in her, but Anna had avoided talking to her friend so she wouldn't have to get a lecture about breaking up with Ethan.

She got home that night and went through the motions of making dinner, cleaning up around the house, and trying to catch up on her reading. But later that night, she had read the same page twice and still couldn't get a handle on the story.

"Well, this is useless," she said aloud to herself, slamming her book closed. "Did I do the wrong thing? Or was it the right thing? How am I supposed to know the difference?'

Memories flooded in as she compared the beginnings of her relationship with Alan with her recent dates with Ethan. Alan had been polite and nice, but when she really thought about it, he never truly seemed like he was listening to her, only pretending to be interested by agreeing with every word she said.

The conversations with Ethan, however, felt sincere. He would gaze at her with his eyes as deep and blue as the vast expanse of the heavens, listening intently as she talked about her dreams, her thoughts, her feelings.

No, there was something much different in her connection with Ethan, something on a deeper level.

"I did," she said to Sammy, who stared up at her wagging his tail. "I did make a mistake. But it's too late now. I don't think there's anything I can do about it. If he really does care about me, then I truly hurt him the other night at the restaurant. I couldn't even explain what was wrong."

She slid open the back door just off the kitchen, which led out onto a small deck with two cushioned chairs and a table with a red umbrella in the center. The night was dark, and she looked up at the stars.

"I wish there was a way I could know for sure," she said, leaning back in her chair.

* * *

ETHAN HAD SPENT THE EVENING WALKING AROUND HIS FARMHOUSE vegetable garden and his small barnyard, where three young sheep nestled in the hay. The sheep were young, and Ethan had found them through an animal rescue group. An elderly couple had become too ill to take care of their farm animals, so the rescue group helped find them new homes. He enjoyed spending time watching the sheep interact and cuddle up together for a good night's sleep. There was something comforting in witnessing the happiness of animals who felt safe in their surroundings.

But Ethan couldn't focus on vegetables or sheep. His mind wandered, as it had for several days, since Anna had driven away in that restaurant parking lot.

"What did I do wrong?" he asked himself aloud.

He walked over to the patio and sat down on a chair next to a wooden table.

"So, we're talking to ourselves now, are we?" teased a woman walking up behind him. She was older, in her mid-fifties, tall and slender with light green eyes and short hair with a silvery tint from its greying locks. "I brought you some tea," she added.

"Louise, thank you. You always think tea will solve everything," said Ethan.

"And is there something to be solved on this clear, quiet night?" she asked.

"You know there is," he answered.

"A young woman who needs time is not a problem to be solved," she said with a reassuring smile. "Love is a confusing and complex thing, and we women need to absorb all its splendor as it happens to us. That takes time."

"I know, and I'm perfectly willing to give her the time she needs. It's just … difficult," Ethan said, taking a sip of the tea Louise had made for him. "This is wonderful, as always," he added.

"Nothing but the best for you," Louise said, smiling. "I've always loved you as a son. Jeffery and I would have loved children of our own." She closed her eyes as memories poured in of her late husband. "But we enjoyed every moment watching you grow up," she added.

"You were always a great mother when my own mom couldn't be around."

"Your parents were busy. There was so much to be done building a business and a life," Louise explained. "You know that yourself now."

"Yes, it didn't take me long to understand that as I got older. They're great parents, but I'm still glad that you've always been there for me, Louise. Thank you." Ethan smiled.

"Ethan, I've known you since you were in diapers, and I'll say one thing for you. I have never once known you to give up on something you truly wanted," said Louise, "especially something this important."

Louise rose and grasped her cup of tea.

"You're right, as always," said Ethan. "And your tea has always gotten the job done as well. It's like a magic remedy somehow. How do you do it?" he asked.

"A woman can't give away ALL her secrets," she laughed as she glided away, her tailored black suit shimmering in the moonlight.

Ethan laughed, set his own cup down on the table, and rested his head back to look up at the stars.

"I'll wait until you're ready, Anna," he said aloud as he noticed a bright star twinkle in the clear sky above.

CHAPTER ELEVEN

After work the next day, Anna pulled into her driveway and noticed something unusual on her front porch. She kept driving into her garage behind her house, closed up the garage, and walked around front to see what it was.

As she turned the corner, she noticed flowers, a large arrangement of spring colors arranged in a basket display.

She trembled.

'Alan wouldn't leave me flowers, would he? They must be from Ethan, but he agreed to give me space. They'd better not be from Alan,' she thought, looking around nervously to see if anyone was nearby. The street was empty.

She took a deep breath and went closer to see who they were from, noticing a small envelope at the top. Inside was a small card with a floral watermark that read, 'Join me for another date, Anna? I promise we'll take things slow. --Ethan.'

She didn't know which emotion she felt more strongly, the relief that Alan wasn't stalking her or the thrill of Ethan asking her out for another date. She smiled and brought the flowers into her house.

Sammy jumped up on the coffee table to take a whiff of the new foliage in the house.

"Those are from Ethan," she said aloud with a smile so wide she was glowing. "But I'm not sure what to do." She decided to call Kelly for advice.

"Can I come over for a few minutes?" Anna asked when she got Kelly on the phone.

"Yes, always. Is something wrong?" Kelly answered in a concerned voice.

"No, I'm okay. I just need to talk real quick."

"About time," Kelly said. "Come on over."

When she arrived at Kelly's house, John was home as well.

"Hi, Anna," he greeted her. "Don't worry about me, I'm cooking dinner and I'll get out of your hair. Want to stay for a bite?"

"I don't want to impose," Anna answered.

"Don't be silly. We have plenty and you're always welcome. I'll set another place and finish up while you two talk."

"Thanks, John," she said. "He's wonderful," Anna told Kelly when he left the room.

"I know," Kelly beamed. "But I want to talk about you. You've been ignoring me all week, girl! What is up with you? Is that disgusting Alan bothering you again?"

"No, that's not it," Anna answered. "Um, I sort of broke up with Ethan."

"You did what!?" Kelly nearly hollered in disbelief.

"Well, I got scared. Really scared."

"About what? Ethan's wonderful."

"Kelly, you've never even met the man," Anna laughed.

"Well, technically no. I guess not. But everything I heard about him is great. And those amazing dates you had were … well, amazing! Why in the world would you break up with that beautiful man?" she asked.

"I don't know. I guess it was the whole Alan thing…"

"That man is definitely NOT Alan…"

"I know, I know. I was stupid. It's just all those memories about Alan came rushing back and something told me that Ethan wasn't being honest with me. I'm not sure what it is at all. I just have this weird feeling about him, and I can't even explain it," Anna said.

"Weird feeling?"

"Yes. Like he's hiding something. I don't know. And you've never met him so you can't really tell me if I'm just imagining things."

"I think it's probably just your imagination, Anna," said Kelly, "but you're right, I haven't technically met him."

"Well, he's asked me out again."

"He has?"

"Yes. And I don't know what to do. I can't shake this nagging feeling that he's hiding something, but whenever I think of him, I just … I don't know. I'm so confused."

"Well, I think you should give him a chance, Anna."

"I know. But I was thinking. I want you to meet him. So maybe our next date could be a double date, if it's okay with you and John. That way, you can both meet him and tell me if I'm being an idiot or not."

"Anna, you are no idiot," laughed Kelly. "I understand. You're being cautious. You weren't cautious with Alan and that put you in an emotional mess. I don't want you to go through anything like that again, either."

"So you'll do it?" Anna asked.

"Yes, and I'm sure John would be happy to help."

"How am I helping?" John asked as he came around the corner. "I'm always happy to help. Tell me how," he laughed.

"We're double dating," explained Kelly.

"Oh, when? This weekend?"

"I think so," answered Anna. "But I have to call and talk to Ethan."

"We'll just go get dinner served and give you some privacy," said Kelly as she and John walked out of the room.

Anna got out her phone and found Ethan in her contacts, clicking on the call button.

"Hello, Anna, I was hoping you'd call," he said when he answered.

"Hi Ethan. I loved the flowers, thank you," said Anna.

"You're very welcome. I hope you don't think I'm rushing you or anything. I just wanted to let you know that I'm still thinking about you, and that we can go out, maybe to the county fair this weekend, and take things as slowly as you need to," he answered.

"Thank you, I appreciate that. I would like to take you up on that, and I have an idea that I hope you'll like," she said.

"What's that?" he asked.

"I'd like to go on a double date with my best friend and her boyfriend. I'd love for you to meet her, she's very important in my life."

"That would be wonderful. So it's a date for the fair?" he asked.

"Yes, I think that's the perfect place to go. Friday evening maybe? They have some great food because there are a bunch of cooking contests. It's not The Trinity Oceana," she laughed, "but it always makes a really great meal."

"That sounds incredible. I'd love to go with you, and meet your friends," he said.

"Wonderful. Meet me at my house around six and we'll all go together," said Anna happily.

"I'll see you then. I'm looking forward to this, Anna," said Ethan.

"Me, too," Anna answered.

Excited, she joined Kelly and John in the kitchen for a great meal, and they all looked forward to the double date that weekend.

CHAPTER TWELVE

Early Friday evening, Ethan arrived and stepped out of his black SUV in front of Anna's house. He was dressed casually for the county fair, in jeans and a dark blue t-shirt that showed off his well-defined muscles. Anna met him at the door wearing a floral sundress and strappy sandals.

"You look incredible, Anna, as always," he said as he took her hand in his.

"Thanks, you too," she said, squeezing his hand. "We're still waiting on Kelly and John. They should be here soon."

"Perfect," said Ethan.

"In the meantime, come on in and we'll have a cup of coffee or something," Anna said, motioning toward the door. Their hands slid away from one another's as they both stepped inside.

"And who is this?" Ethan asked, walking over to pet Sammy on the sofa. "Sammy, right?"

"Yes, that's right!" Anna exclaimed, amazed that he could remember such a detail from their first date.

"I never forget a pet's name," he explained as he scratched Sammy behind his ears.

They laughed, then headed to the kitchen for some coffee.

"How was your day?" Ethan asked her.

"Busy. The kids are always antsy on Fridays waiting for the weekend."

He laughed. "I sure remember that feeling."

"Ethan. I'm so sorry if I hurt you. I'm not sure what it is, but I just felt like I needed to take a step back," Anna said.

"You never have to apologize for needing to take time for your feelings, Anna."

"Thank you," she said.

"Knock, knock," Kelly said at the front door. Only the screen door was closed so that Anna would hear when they arrived.

"Hi!" Anna greeted them excitedly. "Kelly, this is Ethan. Ethan, this is my very best friend in the whole world, Kelly."

"It's a pleasure to meet you," Ethan said, offering a handshake.

"It's so great to finally meet you!" exclaimed Kelly, ignoring his hand and moving in for a quick, friendly hug.

"Hi, I'm John. I just stand here looking great till I hear my name," said John.

They all laughed, and John and Ethan shook hands. "Good to meet you, too," said Ethan.

"Would you like some coffee before we go?" Anna asked.

"We're good, thanks. It's starting to get late, and we'll want a good parking spot," Kelly answered.

"Let's go then," Ethan said. "I'll drive, just tell me where I'm going." They all laughed and headed out the door, piling into Ethan's SUV.

* * *

THE COUNTY FAIR WAS HELD EVERY YEAR IN A NEARBY TOWN CALLED Gratham, which was the county seat. It was your typical rural American celebration, with farm animals, lots of food trucks, chili cook offs and other cooking competitions, a few games and rides for the kids, and a football field converted to a concert venue for local bands. On opening night, the band played classic rock tunes and invited the audience to sing along. Ethan, Anna, and their friends enjoyed the atmosphere, each taking turns in the singalong. Ethan and John ended up in a friendly competition.

"I had no idea you could sing so well," said Anna as the group of friends walked off toward the food concessions.

"Hey, I was better than him," John said, and Kelly playfully elbowed him in the arm. "What? I'm good!" he told her.

"Oh, you're good alright," Kelly said, laughing. "So, what does everyone feel like eating? I'm starved."

"I'm game for anything," Ethan said. "You three are the experts in the best cuisine around these parts."

"Well, there's a fantastic spaghetti cook-off competition that's always delicious," John said. "And it's a charity benefit, too, for the humane society in Bluewater."

"That's true," Kelly agreed. "But please don't make a mess like you always do."

"I thought that's how you eat spaghetti," he said. "It shows how much you love it!"

"Spaghetti it is, then." Ethan laughed.

"Let's go!" Anna said. The three friends headed toward a large, white tent where the spaghetti competition was held.

But before they could reach it, a man came walking toward them, seemingly from out of nowhere.

"Oh, I see you're slutting around again, Miss Anna!" Alan Shangle hollered, sarcastically. He was already right up in her face, smelling of alcohol.

"I don't know you, pal, but that's completely uncalled for," Ethan said calmly.

"I'm not your pal," Alan said, glaring at Ethan. "You'd better get away from my fiancé!"

"I am NOT your fiancé!" Anna exclaimed. "And I never will be. You're drunk. You need to leave me alone before I call the police!" For the first time in her life, Anna stood up to Alan without shaking, without being nervous, and without having to rehearse in her head all the things Kelly practiced with her about being assertive.

"You're nothing! I wouldn't want you anyway! You never did

anything right, and you never did anything, really! I had to do every-thing for you because you were too stupid to think of anything. You... you don't... you aren't–" Alan's words devolved into babbling that didn't make sense.

"Alright buddy, this is a family event," said a security guard who had approached. He was about the same height as Ethan, and he put his arm around Alan to lead him away, since Alan was beginning to stumble with his walking as much as his words.

Anna turned to Ethan. "I'm sorry. I'm so embarrassed," she told him.

"Don't be," he said. "It has nothing to do with you. It's his problem, not yours."

"I know," she said, "but it's still embarrassing."

"Forget about that jerk," Kelly said. "I'm hungry, let's go eat." She smiled to lighten the mood.

"Anna, your friend is brilliant," Ethan said.

"Oh, I'm liking you even more now." Kelly laughed.

"Just waiting for my name, just waiting for my name," John said.

"You're a big goof," said Kelly playfully.

They walked forward into the spaghetti tent to enjoy a good meal.

* * *

THE OPENING DAY OF THE FAIR ALWAYS ENDED WITH AERIAL FIREWORKS in the same football field where the band had played earlier, and the four friends took their seats in the grandstands to watch the show.

As the bright sparks of color exploded in the sky, Ethan reached over and held Anna's hand. She smiled at him, then turned back to the show, which was choreographed to music that boomed from the loudspeakers nearby.

Ethan's gaze stayed on Anna for a few minutes as he thought about the earlier encounter with Alan. 'She was with a man who didn't trust her, who had no confidence in her,' he thought to himself. 'By not telling her, I'm treating her no better than that sorry jerk of a guy. I need to tell her.'

The finale was impressive, with seemingly endless fireworks bursting into the sky on top of each other until a final burst was let go by a huge flower-like explosion of color that covered the sky.

Anna turned to Ethan with excitement in her eyes as the show concluded.

"Anna, would you like to see my farmhouse tomorrow?" Ethan asked.

"Yes, yes, I'd love to!" she exclaimed, the last of the fireworks' sparks still reflecting with a twinkle in her emerald eyes.

CHAPTER THIRTEEN

ANNA WAS EXCITED as she got ready to head over to Ethan's farmhouse the next morning. She had heard a lot of talk about the materials Ethan had purchased for the renovations from people in the town, but because it was out in the country on several acres and the house was in the back obscured by trees, most people hadn't seen the results of the upgrades.

She dressed casually, in a green t-shirt and comfortable jeans, dressing up the look with some of her favorite gold earrings and a necklace that she'd bought on one of the many shopping trips with Kelly.

She gave Sammy one last pet, locked up the house, and went to her garage. She pulled out her car and looked into her rearview mirror to be sure her garage door closed. As she looked back toward the street ahead, she noticed a car driving by slowly.

Instantly she recognized the light blue sedan driven by Alan Shangle, and her hands started shaking. Their eyes met as he passed, and his facial expression was as cold as stone.

Anna took a deep breath after he passed and pulled out of her driveway in the opposite direction. She would have to turn around a few blocks up, but she didn't want to follow Alan or have him know which way she was going. As she pulled out of town, the distinctive blue car was nowhere to be seen, and she drove off toward Ethan's farmhouse in the country.

By the time she arrived, she had shaken off the fear and become excited about seeing what Ethan had done to fix up his house.

She read the address on the mailbox, 916, and was sure she was in the right place as she pulled into the long and winding tree-lined driveway. The property was a mixture of pastureland and thick brush, with a meandering stream running through its center where the natural vegetation grew high. The trees lining the driveway were mature, having been erected decades ago by a previous owner.

The house itself was very small but charming, with a deck in front opening to a gravel area for parking. There were small outbuildings scattered throughout the property. Anna could see that Ethan had recently installed new siding, giving the little farmhouse a clean and modern appeal.

Ethan stepped out of the house and down the deck's steps to meet Anna at her car.

"This is adorable!" she exclaimed as she exited her vehicle.

"Thanks, I'm glad you like it," Ethan answered, smiling and taking her by the hand. "I'll give you the grand tour."

"I can't wait," she said.

The front door opened into a small, pleasant living room, with polished wooden floors and light grey walls with wood trim, furnished in a style that reflected its rural country charm. The kitchen and small dining area were off to the side, with a few more doors in a small hallway that Anna assumed were bedrooms and a bathroom. The kitchen had modern cabinets and appliances with a slate grey stone floor.

"It's all so lovely," said Anna as they sat down at the small dining room table. "You've done an amazing job with the place."

"Thanks. I still need to show you the outside. Would you like something to drink?" he asked.

"Nothing yet, thanks. I'd love to see everything first, if that's okay," Anna answered.

"Absolutely. Wait till you see the barn!" Ethan exclaimed.

They went out the back door, where a black golf cart waited by a stone patio with a brick fireplace and a small table with an umbrella and two chairs.

"It's quicker to get around this way," he laughed.

"It's adorable," she said.

The first stop was the vegetable garden, and Anna was impressed. It was late spring, so the plants were still maturing. The large garden was organized in perfect rows with a drip watering system perfectly covering the plants so there would be no wasted water.

"This is very nice," Anna said. "I can't wait to harvest some."

"Thank you. In California, we'd be farther along in the growing season, but I like the snowy winters as well."

"Me, too. It gives you a sense of the cycle of life in the world," she said.

"I agree."

The next stop was the barn with the young sheep, and Anna nearly squealed with delight at the adorable animals running around playfully.

"Can I pet them?" she asked.

"Of course. I've been spending more time with them so they get used to people."

Ethan opened the gate for her, and they both went inside the barnyard enclosure. The sheep seemed to like people, coming right up to Anna while she held her hand out to pet them. She laughed as she watched them play, but then took a step back without looking and felt herself slip. Ethan turned and noticed just as she started to fall, reaching out to grab her. Then he lost his balance, and they both ended up on the hay of the barnyard floor, Ethan on top of Anna. They gazed into each other's eyes for a moment until the sheep ran up and started nuzzling the couple. They both laughed and Ethan got up, offering both hands to Anna as she rose and dusted off her clothes.

"Well, I'm a mess now," she laughed.

"I'm so sorry," he said. "I should have warned you that it gets slippery in here. Are you alright?"

"I'm fine, and it's okay. They're so cute I wasn't paying attention."

"Let's get you in the house to clean up," Ethan said as he helped her out to the golf cart.

"Where's your dog and cat?" Anna asked on the ride back.

"Oh," Ethan said. "I'll have to introduce you later."

Anna wondered for a moment why his dog wouldn't be by his side, knowing that a cat with free run of a farm would probably be out of sight. She let it go and looked at her shirt, which was a mess of mud and stuck bits of hay and probably manure.

"I think I need to run home and change before lunch," she said.

"Okay. Yes, I'm so sorry," Ethan agreed.

"Don't be. I'm having a wonderful time. I just don't want to stink like manure all night," she laughed.

"Let me get you a towel or two for your car," Ethan said when they got to the house. They walked through the back door, and he went to a closet at the end of the small hallway, grabbing a couple of soft grey towels and then walking her out the front door.

"The stitching is lovely," Anna noticed as she took the towels from him.

"My mother always told me to buy quality towels," he explained, smiling. "I could always give you something to change into if you'd like to shower here," he added.

"I think I'd disappear in one of your shirts," she laughed.

He started to say something else but stopped himself, since she was already in her car with her seatbelt on.

"I'll be back in just a few minutes," she said.

"I'll have lunch ready for you," he answered.

"That will be lovely. I can't wait to talk to you more, Ethan."

"It's a lunch date then," he said, smiling as he squeezed her hand before they parted, and she drove off.

CHAPTER FOURTEEN

Both Ethan and Anna had showered and changed when she returned to the farm. The table was set with elegant placemats and a vase of lovely colorful wildflowers, and the smell of fresh bread was in the air.

"I hope you didn't go to a lot of trouble," Anna said.

"It was nothing," he said with a smile.

It was already well into the afternoon. Being hungry, they both dug into the delicious meal and ate for a few minutes in silence.

"I was starving," Anna laughed. "I hope you don't think I eat like that every day. Everything was so delicious."

He laughed. "I wouldn't mind if you did. It's good to have a healthy appetite."

"That bread was amazing," she said. "You didn't have to go to the trouble."

"Oh, it was no trouble at all. It's my mom's old recipe, adapted for a bread machine. They both laughed.

"Well, it was delicious all the same."

"Thank you," said Ethan. "How about some coffee out on the patio?" he suggested.

"That sounds wonderful, thank you," answered Anna. Soon they were both outside on the padded chairs, looking out at the vast expanse of rolling green hills that met the clear, bright blue sky.

"Do you still have work with the kids out for summer?" Ethan asked. The county fair had marked the first weekend without school for the students of Belleville.

"I still have some grading and planning to wrap up, but I'm almost done for the summer. I don't have a summer school class this year because I decided to take a break," said Anna. "How is your work going?"

"It's going well," answered Ethan. "I'd like to show you some things about my work a little later, if that's okay."

"I'd be delighted," she said.

"Oh, here's Milo," Ethan said as a tabby cat approached. The cat came up to Ethan and rubbed against his leg. "It must be feeding time," he laughed.

"Oh, he's adorable," Anna said, reaching out her hand. Milo walked right up to her for a pet. "Where's your dog? What was his name again?" she asked.

"Teddy, and you'll be meeting him shortly," explained Ethan.

Anna thought about asking why the dog wasn't there, but she was too distracted petting the cat, who had jumped up on her lap.

"Tell me about your ideas for an animal rescue," said Ethan.

Delighted, she went on to explain how she planned to open a shelter with huge cages that were more like rooms in homes than cages. "That way," she explained, "the animals that aren't normally adopted, like strays, will be more comfortable in an indoor home setting. I'm hoping that helps them. I'd have plenty of people volunteer, including my students, so the animals are never without human company. And now that I've seen your barn, I think I want to add something like that for rescue horses and other farm animals that need help. I guess that's a lot, but a girl can dream," she said, gazing into Ethan's blue eyes.

"You absolutely can," said Ethan. "And I think those are great ideas."

"Really?"

"Yes, absolutely. Milo here was a rescue, and I wanted to take all of them home when I saw all the cats and dogs in those cages," explained Ethan. "I guess I've had some of the same ideas you've had about helping animals."

"That's wonderful," said Anna with a smile. "It seems we're a lot alike."

"Yes, we are," he said, gazing into her emerald eyes. Would you like to take a walk? I promise we won't fall into sheep manure this time," he laughed.

"I'd love to," she said.

They strolled over to the creek, where Anna was surprised to find a stone pathway leading through the foliage. It seemed to stretch for miles and looked very new.

"Did you add this?" she asked.

"Yes. I like to take a walk along the creek or ride my bike through here," he explained.

"That must have been expensive," she said. 'Too expensive,' she thought to herself as she kept walking.

They reached a point where the angle of the land, combined with some natural rocks, created a small waterfall. The stone path widened here, and there was a small bench over to the side.

"I love it here. Care to sit down for a few?" Ethan asked.

"I'd love to," she answered.

They sat for a few minutes, chatting more about the property and the lunch he had cooked, then they reminisced about the dinner and the play they'd attended on their second date.

"It was wonderful," she said, and he put his arm around her shoulders.

"I agree," he said softly. They gazed at each other dreamily, and both moved in closer until their lips met. Anna parted her lips and he deepened the kiss, bringing his other arm up to hold her close. The breeze blew gently around them as they melted into one another, reluctantly pulling apart after a few minutes. He slid his hand into hers and looked into her eyes.

"Anna, my feelings for you have grown very deep. I know that it's soon, but I need you to know how I feel," he said.

"I feel the same way, Ethan. I know I said I needed time, and I do, but I can't pretend I'm not feeling something wonderful happening here," she said with a smile.

"Part of our growing relationship is growing trust, so there's something I need to show you," said Ethan.

"What is it?" she asked.

"It's back at the house."

Anna couldn't imagine what he would want to show her, but she was hoping that it was somewhere in his bedroom. She had already made up her mind that she would plunge into this relationship with all her heart, hoping it would work out in the end. Alan, after all, was certainly no Ethan.

Heading through the back door, they entered near the table where they'd recently had lunch. The table and the entire kitchen had been cleared and cleaned.

"What the…" said Anna. She didn't mean to say it aloud, but Ethan had been with her, so there had been no time for him to clean up rather than quickly putting the dishes in the sink.

"It's okay," he said as he led her into a small room at the back of the hallway. When he opened the door, she was stunned at the elaborate marble walls and flooring. The entire room had rails around it in shimmering brass.

"Here, hold onto the sides," he said, and the whole room started shifting, moving down beneath the small, charming old farmhouse.

It was an elevator.

CHAPTER FIFTEEN

Finally, the elevator stopped, so gently that Anna barely felt it. The doors in front of her slid open silently, revealing a slate-blue marble hallway decorated with lush greenery and a huge waterfall that seems to rain droplets from the sky. At first, Anna imagined that they'd stepped into the sunlight, because the hallway was lit with a warm, natural glow, but she realized that it must be some type of lighting.

"What… what is this?" Anna's voice hit the air as a whisper, out of breath from the shock of the sudden change of scenery.

"Good morning, Mr. Greenfield," said a woman walking by. "And hello, miss, it's so nice to see you here." She was a woman of about 50, with a warm, friendly smile that felt like that of Anna's own mother. She wore a well-tailored lavender suit that looked like silk.

"Hello," Anna managed to answer, smiling in amazement. She felt Ethan's touch move smoothly from her hand to the small of her back, where it warmed her as he led her forward.

"Hi, Louise. This is Anna," said Ethan, looking deeply into Anna's emerald eyes, speaking more to her than to Louise. Louise smiled broadly and walked away, leaving Anna to marvel at her astonishing new surroundings.

"These paintings, they're exquisite. I've never seen a landscape so realistic and beautiful. The lighting of the sunset in that one is breath-taking," she managed to say.

"You only notice paintings?" Ethan laughed with understanding. He imagined the level of surprise she must feel when only a few steps ago she was walking through an old farmhouse.

"Oh, I notice a lot more than that. I'm just trying to figure this all out. What is this?" she answered, finally getting her breath back.

"This is my real home, and you're the first woman I've ever shown it to," he said.

"I just saw a woman there... "

"You're special." He stopped and they shared a tender look before Ethan broke away from their gaze. "Come on, this is just the main hallway."

"There's more?" Anna asked.

He laughed. "So much more. This is only the beginning."

He led her down the hallway and Anna marveled at the exquisite architecture hidden underneath a small and common looking farmhouse. The hallway ceiling appeared to be windows opening up into the sunshine, but that was impossible. Anna was sure she hadn't seen any buildings with windows coming up out of the ground when she was up in the garden outside.

"It looks like the sun," she thought, not realizing she had said it aloud.

"It's a special type of artificial sunlight developed by a start-up company in Hawaii. Amazing how realistic it is, isn't it? It even lets off the right kind of rays so that it feels like sunshine even underground," Ethan explained.

"It's amazing," she said. They walked on to the end of the hallway, and all the while Anna looked around, stunned at the sights.

They entered a new room at the end that seemed to be an expansive living room. It was tastefully decorated with various shades of green, with overstuffed, comfortable furniture and polished woodwork that looked like cherry wood. The walls were made of an emerald-colored marble with wood trim. A woman dusted a table in the corner, and a man walked through carrying a tray of some kind.

"Who are these people?" Anna mumbled.

"Good morning, Mr. Greenfield," said the man and woman, seemingly in unison, both smiling brightly then continuing with their tasks.

"Good morning, Betty, Hans. Good to see you both," answered Ethan.

"Wait a minute," said Anna as she stopped in her tracks. "This is some sort of underground mansion. You're rich. You're like a billionaire or something?"

"Something like that, yes," Ethan answered with a smile.

"What? How is that possible? We're … you're from Belleville. Well not exactly. But I'm from Belleville. There's never been anybody with any real money in Belleville. We're in the middle of nowhere. Out on a farm. There are sheep upstairs. In a barn. Sheep sitting in hay. Are you serious with this? This is a real place? How… why–" Anna couldn't put any words together in her head that made any sense at all. None of this made any sense.

"Maybe we'd better sit down so I can explain before I show you the rest," Ethan said, leading her to the sofa. His hand hadn't left her back since they stepped off the elevator, so she felt his warmth leave as he removed it so she could sit down. Instantly she missed his touch, that comforting warmth. Her feelings added to her confusion about her surroundings.

"There's even more?" she questioned, still in shock.

"Yes," he laughed, "but let's talk for a bit first. I guess I'll start from the beginning."

"That works," she said slowly with a light breath, still taking in her surroundings.

"My grandfather was from Belleville. My mom's dad. His father before him owned a store here, but Grandad left town when he was old enough because he wanted to live in the city, so the family ended up in LA, where he met my grandma and my mom eventually met my dad. Grandad worked hard, and when he earned enough money, he bought this farm so he'd always feel close to home, even hundreds of miles away."

"Okay," said Anna, listening intently.

"My parents never liked the country either, but when they inherited the place, they kept it for me in case I ever wanted it. So I grew up in Los Angeles."

"Yes, California, you had told me that…" she managed to say.

"Yes, LA. My father made some good investments in real estate, and I took over the business when I got old enough. I made some lucky stock choices, some digital investments, and that all went well."

"So that's the investing and property management you do," said Anna.

"Yes," answered Ethan.

"So why are you here hiding under a barn full of sheep in a mansion?" Anna asked with a confused look on her face. Ethan wished he could explain faster to spare her the mixed emotions.

"I grew up with money and added more to it when I followed Dad into business. I wanted to do something with my money that mattered. In LA, everyone always watched what you did and thought you were crazy if you helped people, but that's all I ever wanted to do. No one ever talks to you just to be nice. They all have a hidden agenda. I didn't want to play that game anymore, so I wanted to find a way to be myself again." His sky-blue eyes looked into hers intensely, speaking to her beyond the words. Something inside Anna stirred and understood.

"You wanted to be more than money," she said.

"Exactly. To me, money is a resource for good, but so many people use it for evil, so many people are greedy, and so many see you only one way when you're a CEO."

"A CEO…" Anna repeated.

"In my family's company, yes. But I wanted to find real happiness. I wanted to find love," he smiled as he looked into her eyes. "I wanted to find you."

Anna's lips parted slightly with surprise, then closed and spread into a smile. "And here I am," was all she could manage to say.

He leaned in, his arms wrapping around her as his lips met hers. She closed her eyes and melted into his touch, sliding her hands around his muscular frame. They kissed, enveloping into each other in a world all their own as time stood still, until he broke away softly and they both took a deep breath.

"So, do you want to see the rest?" he asked with a grin.

"Let's go," she said, smiling with a glow of happiness.

CHAPTER SIXTEEN

ANNA AND ETHAN WALKED ON, meandering through the underground mansion's many rooms and hallways. Ethan had shown her several different rooms, each extravagant yet tasteful, with quality furnishings and finishes showcasing a minimalistic and contemporary styling.

"You'll love this room," Ethan said with a smile as the door slid open. Like many main entrances to the larger rooms, it slid quietly open and disappeared into the wall as they approached.

Inside was a vast living room, but it wasn't furnished just for humans. Instead, huge, oversized dog beds and cat trees were everywhere, and the walls were a playground of steps, landings, and hanging baskets where a tabby cat lounged, looking disinterestedly at the new intruders in the room. Around the outside were box-like enclosures.

"Oh, my goodness!" exclaimed Anna as a large German Shepherd approached her, tail wagging.

"This is Teddy," Ethan said. "And this is why I didn't introduce you before. He was waiting in this room to surprise you."

"Oh, this is a wonderful surprise," she said, kneeling down and hugging the friendly dog. "The cats don't mind him? How many cats are there?" she asked, looking up at the play wall.

"Milo grew up around Teddy, so he's used to him. I'm afraid this is all just for the two of them right now. I built it so I could get some more cats eventually, but for now it's all his when he's indoors. He's spoiled," he laughed.

"I'll say," she said with a grin. "What are these boxes?"

"I keep the cat food and litter boxes in there so Teddy doesn't get into them. Milo gets in from behind, where the dog can't reach. Most of these are empty for later when I get more cats," Ethan explained.

"This is wonderful," Anna said.

"It's one of my favorite rooms. But I have more to show you," he said.

A young woman walked in dressed in jeans and a t-shirt, carrying a box of cleaning supplies.

"Hello, Tara," Ethan said to her. "Tara, this is Anna. Anna, Tara," he said as he gestured toward each of the women. "Tara originally brought Teddy to me from a rescue. She still spends a lot of time with him."

"Hi, Tara," said Anna.

"Hi," said Tara. "I'm still really attached to him. I fell in love with this dog the second I saw him in that cage."

"I don't blame you," Anna said, standing up. She had been petting the dog the whole time.

"I have a lot to show you, if that's okay," said Ethan. "I knew you'd love this room."

"I do! And Tara, it's so nice to meet you," said Anna.

"Same here," answered Tara as she turned to pet the German Shepherd.

Ethan took Anna's hand and led her out the room.

"Do you like to swim?" Ethan asked as he opened the next door across the hallway. Anna didn't have time to answer before she was awestruck by the pool and exercise room. Half the room had professional gym equipment, and the other half was devoted to a crystal-clear lap pool. toward the back behind the pool, she noticed an octagonal hot tub.

"The door in the back leads to a changing room and showers, and in there, there's a small steam room that I use to relax sometimes," said Ethan.

Anna stared in amazement. "This whole place is huge," was all she managed to say.

"The entire compound down here runs roughly the size of the property. I designed it so it wouldn't interfere with the creek bed and some other natural features above, so there are some gaps rather than having a single structure," Ethan explained.

"it's all so … overwhelming," she said.

"I know, and I understand. It's a lot to spring on you at once, but I needed to share this with you, Anna." He turned and faced her, taking her hand in his. "I know you don't want to rush things, and neither do I, but I'm falling in love with you, Anna, and part of building that relationship is trusting you with knowing my real life."

Tears started to form, making her emerald eyes glisten with the reflection of the light of the pool room. "I'm falling in love with you, too, Ethan," she said.

He wrapped his arms around her, pulling her in close. Her hands slid across his back as she felt his well-formed muscles under his shirt. They held each other tightly for a moment, then he pulled back gently before moving toward her again, his lips meeting hers. Their bodies melted together as they stood near the center of the room, time standing still once more in the silence of the vast expanse of the underground mansion. He pulled away again, sliding his hand back into hers.

"I can't and won't rush you, Anna," he told her.

"I know," she said in a whisper, still under the spell of his kiss.

"We've been walking for a while," he said, "do you need a drink or anything?"

She hadn't even noticed the time pass, but the sheer size of the mansion called for quite a bit of walking for the tour. The temperature in the rooms was perfect, and the air felt clear and crisp, so she hadn't thought of needing to stop for a drink until Ethan mentioned it.

"I think so, yes," she answered.

"There's a lounge room nearby. Let's go there," he suggested.

"Lead the way," she said, smiling at him, her eyes still twinkling from the tears of joy.

The lounge resembled a private club, and Ethan offered Anna a seat in a barstool before walking behind the bar. "What'll you have, pretty lady?" he asked with a laugh.

Anna laughed with him. "I'll just have a lemon-lime soda, if you have it."

"Of course," he answered.

He took two glasses out from under the counter and put them under a dispenser that plopped sphere-shaped ice into the glasses, then filled them with soda from a fountain, handing one to Anna. Then he walked around and sat in the stool next to hers.

"To us," he said. "Going slow," he added with a smile.

"To us," she said, and their glasses clinked together before each took a sip. "So, tell me more about this place."

"I've known about the farm all my life, but I'd never been here before recently. My parents hated the country, and I'll never understand why, so they gave it to me," he said as Anna listened intently. "It really started out as a crazy idea when I was younger. One of my dad's clients showed me his underground bunker out in the desert in Nevada. He was a great guy but a little eccentric."

Anna raised her eyebrows and grinned.

"Yes, I suppose so am I," he continued. "I just thought it was the coolest thing I'd ever seen, and in the back of my mind since that day, I always knew I'd build something like that of my own."

"This is much more than a bunker," Anna said.

He laughed. "Yes, that's true as well. I guess the idea just kept growing like a seed until I had these huge plans in my head. When I got older and they gave me this property out in the country, I knew it was the perfect place to do it. I was so tired of the city life and all the social circles my parents ran around in. I just wanted to do what I wanted to with my money, without the paparazzi snapping pictures every time I stepped out my door or people constantly coming to me asking for money."

"That would get tiring," Anna agreed.

"Yes. So I thought I'd go ahead with my dream and build my idea out here."

"How on earth did you get it done without anyone knowing?" Anna asked.

"Well, I let it be known that I was doing renovations, and I was," he laughed, "so when equipment showed up here, no one really noticed. There aren't any neighbors out here. The guys who did the work weren't from around here. They stayed in the house and some tents in the back during construction. They were all well paid, with lifetime benefits for their families so they wouldn't disclose my secret."

"That's amazing," she said.

"Now I get to live my dream. And I never in a million years expected to find you in the tiny town nearby. It's like you drew me here," said Ethan.

"I guess there is such a thing as fate," Anna said.

They continued talking for hours, all through a gourmet dinner they shared in one of the dining rooms and late into the evening. She talked about her teaching career and more about her dreams of running an animal shelter. He told her stories about the people who worked at the mansion, his life in the city, and his business.

"Are you still the CEO?" she asked.

"Yes. That kind of business can be run from anywhere. I'll show you my offices ..." he paused, noticing the fatigue on her face. "I'm so sorry, Anna. It's so late and I've kept you up almost all night."

"It's okay," she said. "I love talking to you. It feels so natural and comforting that I lost track of time. I guess I should get home."

"I'd hate for you to drive when you're this tired. I have plenty of spare rooms down here, and you're welcome to stay. I would never rush you into anything, Anna," he added when he noticed her look of concern. "We'll have separate rooms."

Anna was too tired to disagree and had dreaded the thought of driving home that late. There was no rush to get home, since she had put out extra food and water for her cat, secretly hoping that she wouldn't be home that night anyway. A big part of her wanted Ethan to sweep her off her feet so she could nestle into his muscular body until they woke up in each other's arms the next morning. Another part of her cautioned herself to let things happen slowly. Staying at the mansion in her own room was somewhat of a compromise, for now.

"That sounds wonderful," she said.

"I'll show you to your room," Ethan said with a smile.

CHAPTER SEVENTEEN

ANNA AWOKE THE NEXT MORNING, her groggy eyes slowly opening in the morning light. Her hand reached to her side where normally she would give Sammy his first morning pet, but there was nothing beside her on the bed. She hazily thought of the dream she'd had the night before of a fabulous mansion and a handsome man, but as her eyes focused, she realized that her dream was indeed quite real.

Her room certainly wasn't her own. The bed was huge with a cherry wood frame and luxurious green canopy, with a matching comforter and feather-soft sheets enveloping her body. She sat up and looked around, noticing the stunning detail of the wood trim on the walls, chic original artwork, and simple yet elegant furnishings in the room.

"Oh, my goodness," she said aloud to herself, with a twinge of anxiety growing in her chest. It was a feeling Anna experienced often in her life, feeling as though she had done something wrong or was going to get in trouble when she had done nothing to be anxious about. It was part of the reason why Alan's control over her had been so pervasive. He had sensed her irrational fears and used them to his advantage.

Yet Alan clearly wasn't there in this luxurious, expansive room.

And neither was Ethan, whose gentlemanly conduct had led last night to a gentle yet passionate kiss at her door and nothing else.

Ethan. Thoughts of him came rushing into her mind, along with the shocking revelation he had shared with her the night before.

'Oh, great,' she thought to herself. 'Now I have to worry about whether I'm only after his money.'

She rose out of bed, wearing the nightshirt she had found in the room's closet. She was about to change into her clothes she'd worn the day before when she heard a knock on the door.

"Anna," called Louise, the lovely older lady she had seen the night before. She cracked the door just enough to be heard. "It's Louise, and I'm alone. May I come in? I've brought you some clothes."

"Yes, hi. Come in, Louise," answered Anna.

The woman entered, wearing a beautifully tailored beige suit. Anna smiled, suddenly realizing why Ethan's suit had such an impeccable fit on their second date. Ethan must have a private tailor.

"We have a few ladies working here, so we always have extra clothes on hand. I thought these might fit you so you wouldn't have to wear the same thing today," said Louise.

"Thank you, those are lovely," said Anna as Louise hung up the outfit. It was a form-fitting, light green linen dress that looked like a perfect fit.

"I thought this would work best with the shoes you wore yesterday," said Louise.

"It's perfect," said Anna with a smile.

"The chef has prepared a wonderful breakfast. I hope you'll join us," Louise added.

"Yes, I'd love to," Anna answered.

"I'll leave you to get dressed."

"Louise?"

"Yes?" said Louise, turning before she reached the door.

"Why is it light in here when we're underground?"

"Oh, yes, that's always surprising for me every morning as well. The lighting system in here imitates natural light, including a sunrise.

You can program it to earlier or later to suit your tastes," Louise explained.

"That's amazing. Everything here is amazing."

Louise smiled. "When you're ready, just walk straight down this hallway to your left," she said as she walked out the door.

Anna loved the dress, which fit her form perfectly and accentuated all her features, including her eyes and the red tint of her hair. Her mind wandered as she looked around at all the beautiful artwork in the room.

'His wealth is a problem,' she thought. Not long ago, she had questioned how her future with Ethan could work, uncertain about where things had gone wrong with Alan. She could not deny that some questions remained in her mind. Was she truly falling in love with Ethan, or was it more of the imagined love that she had experienced in the beginning with Alan? Now, new complications and new questions entered her mind. Would she ignore any red flags that might arise in their relationship because he is a billionaire? How could she ever be certain that what she feels for Ethan is true love?

The thoughts haunted her as she exited her room and walked down the hall to breakfast.

Ethan rose as she approached. "Good morning," he greeted her. "Did you sleep well?"

"Very," she answered. She smiled, but there was a twinge of uncertainty in her face. Ethan sensed it.

"Is something the matter?" he asked.

"We do need to talk, but I don't want this beautiful breakfast going to waste, so let's enjoy that first," she said.

"Our chef's name is Benjamin, and he does make a fabulous presentation," Ethan explained. "He created that wonderful dinner last night as well."

Anna remembered the delicious dishes they had enjoyed the night before during their long conversation. And now, delectable breakfast foods were displayed on the table in front of her. She noticed how fresh and colorful the fruit appeared. "We don't get exotic fruit around here that looks that incredible," she observed.

"We have a team that procures our food from the freshest sources," Ethan said. "We buy from small farms that need the support and fly it in. We buy large quantities, and send most of it to charities."

"That's amazing," she said.

They ate slowly and quietly, with little conversation other than exchanging small pleasantries about the chef's dishes.

As they finished, Ethan said, "Anna, I understand how overwhelming all this is. I know it will take some time to soak in."

"Yes, it will. And I do need some time, not just for this, but to work through some of my own emotions. On top of everything I was worried about before, now I have to be sure that my feelings are genuine and not affected by wealth and all this incredible stuff happening down here," she said as she waved her hands around to indicate the underground mansion.

"I'm so sorry," Ethan said. "I should have given you more time. I just needed you to know about this …"

"No, no. It's fine, I understand that you didn't want to keep me in the dark anymore, and I appreciate the honesty," Anna said.

"There are still some other things to show you that can answer some questions," Ethan added.

"Not today, please, Ethan," she said. "Let me go home and have some time to absorb all this part first."

"Okay," he agreed reluctantly. "I did promise that we'd take things slowly."

"Thank you. And thank you so much for this incredible breakfast. Tell the chef he is amazing for me, please."

"I will," Ethan said

.

They both rose and walked through the hallways to the marble elevator, then they both stepped in.

"This is the only entrance?" she asked.

"There are several entrances, and an underground parking garage. This one is just closest to where your car is parked right now."

"Incredible," she said, the word trailing off into a whisper.

When they reached the top, they exited the small country farmhouse and he walked her to her car.

"I'll call you later," she said.

"I'll talk to you then," he answered. Ethan moved forward, grasping both of Anna's hands. "We have forever, Anna. Take the time you need to sort your feelings."

"Thank you," she said, moving closer. He let go of her hands and moved his arms around her, holding her close. Their lips met and she let herself melt into him as she felt an undeniable spark that simply had to be a genuine love. But she had to be sure. She'd been hurt before.

"I'll see you later, Ethan," she said as they parted. She couldn't bear to say the word 'goodbye.'

"See you, Anna," he answered, then she got in her car and drove away.

CHAPTER EIGHTEEN

Anna walked into her house, threw her keys and purse down on the table, and collapsed into her living room sofa. Her mind had been racing as she drove home, trying to sort out the differences between her relationships with Alan and Ethan. She had felt wonderful being with Alan at the beginning, and she was feeling wonderful now at the beginning with Ethan. Would things go bad for her and Ethan in the same way it did for her and Alan?

The problem was that she just didn't know. "I can't go through all that ever again," she said aloud to Sammy, who had jumped onto her lap, purring. "You're no help. You act all loving and all you want is more food," she laughed as she got up and headed to the kitchen.

Looking at her phone, she saw a string of texts from Kelly. Most of them asked if she was home yet.

'Home,' she texted back.

'About time!' came the quick answer. 'Things must have gone well!' Kelly had followed up the last statement with a smiley face emoji.

'It wasn't that,' Anna answered, laughing to herself. 'I was too tired to drive home.'

'Right, sure,' Kelly texted back, and Anna smiled.

Anna thought about calling her friend, but she realized that she and Ethan had never talked about telling anyone else about the mansion. She assumed that she would have to keep it a secret. Suddenly, the thought came to her that she wouldn't be able to tell Kelly--or even her parents--anything about her entire experience at the mansion. She felt deflated. She had always relied on Kelly's unwavering friendship. Since they were kids, Anna and Kelly had been inseparable, and they always told each other everything.

"I can't tell her a word about this," Anna said aloud. "How will I be able to stand that?" She pondered the thought more as she slipped out of the linen dress and into more casual clothes. She hung the dress and stared at it for a moment. It was the one tangible item that told her that the whole underground mansion experience was real.

But her thoughts returned to wondering about Ethan and worrying that she couldn't share her feelings with Kelly. As she often did when she was upset, Anna started cleaning her house. She scrubbed it from room to room, top to bottom, although it was already fairly clean. She wouldn't have to think of anything if she could focus on her work. Hours later, she noticed it was dark outside and was surprised at how long she had spent on the project. She realized that she was exhausted. She put away her cleaning gear, changed into her nightgown, and went off to bed.

THE NEXT MORNING, ANNA WOKE UP RESTED BUT STILL WORRIED. Another day had dawned, and she still didn't know what to do.

She was making herself breakfast when her phone rang.

"Hello?" she said as she answered it, not paying attention to the phone number on the screen.

"Hi, Anna," said a familiar voice on the other line.

"Alan," she said cautiously, wondering why in the world he would call.

"I know I'm not your favorite person to talk to, but I wanted to apologize for some of the things I've said and done recently."

"Okay," Anna said hesitantly.

"We had something special before, and I'm just still in shock about losing it. I hope that I really didn't lose that special love completely, Anna, and that we can be friends, at least for now," said Alan. "Maybe we could go somewhere together, like get a drink or something."

"I... I don't know, Alan. You've done some things that friends would never do, and I don't know whether I can forget about all that right now."

"I know," said Alan. "I just wanted you to know that and was hoping I could see you. But I do understand. I'll give you time. Bye, Anna," he said, and hung up the phone.

'What in the world was that?' she thought as she hung up. She went to the window to look outside. She had seen him drive by slowly just the other day, and the look on his face had been so fierce and cold. Now he was being so kind and polite. It just added to her confusion about Ethan.

"Give me time," she said to herself. "It's the same thing Ethan says."

The call from Alan jarred her. Once again, memories came flooding back. It had begun so innocently when they were in high school. She'd never forget the first time he invited her to the prom. It was their first date, and it was spectacular. She had spent a week shopping, trying to pick out the perfect dress, and had finally decided on a deep blue strapless gown with beautiful sparkling stitching. It made her look older and more mature, which at 16 was an important feature. Her mom had taken her to a salon in Bluewater for makeup and hairstyling, and she had felt like a princess.

Suddenly she wondered whether she was feeling like a princess once again. After all, Ethan was so gorgeous with his tall, muscular body and those chiseled features that gave him such a handsome face. And he was rich, a billionaire in fact, with an endlessly huge, extravagant underground mansion and servants everywhere. What woman wouldn't feel like a princess?

"But is it real?" Anna asked herself. "How much of this is real, and how much is just a crazy fantasy? And how on earth will I ever know the difference?"

She returned to the half-cooked breakfast on the stove. She'd turned everything off when she got the phone call, and she didn't even feel like eating now. How could she live a life where she couldn't even talk to her best friend in the world--or her parents--about everything happening with Ethan? How could he put her in a position where she would have to make that kind of choice, between him and everyone else she loved? She was beginning to think that there was no way she could ever be with him.

Even though that feeling of love for him in her heart was so strong.

"I just can't do this. It's not fair to me or him," she told herself.

She picked up the phone and dialed.

CHAPTER NINETEEN

"Hello?" The sound of Ethan's voice as he answered the phone made her heart flutter, but Anna was intent on breaking up with him. She couldn't live a secret life where she couldn't even confide in her best friend.

"Hi, Ethan," she said. "We need to talk."

"Of course," he answered. "Would you like to meet somewhere?"

"No, no I need to say this all right now."

"Need to say what? Anna, what's wrong?" Ethan asked.

"I can't date you anymore. I know this is sudden, and I'm so sorry," she blurted out.

"What … Why, Anna?"

"I just can't do this. I just can't. But you don't need to worry, I'll never reveal your secret to anyone," she said.

"I don't care about that, Anna," he said. "It's you I care about. What is the 'this' that you can't do?"

"This, this whole thing. I'm so sorry. I can't keep all this from my best friend, my parents. I just can't," said Anna.

"Anna, I never said that you couldn't …"

"I know. You thought I could handle this, but I just can't. I'm so sorry, Ethan," she said.

"There are still so many things I need to tell you, to show you, Anna."

"It's going to have to stay that way. It's already hard just with what I already know."

"But Anna …" he pleaded.

"I'm sorry, Ethan. Goodbye," she said, hanging up the phone before she could hear what he said next. Instantly she regretted the decision. She threw the phone to the side and dove into her bed, tears pouring out like rain from the sky. Her heart felt heavy and weak, and her entire body trembled as she buried her face in her pillow and let her emotions take over.

* * *

THE PHONE WENT DEAD BEFORE HE COULD SAY ANYMORE, AND ETHAN wasn't sure if Anna had even heard him tell her that he loved her.

"Anna," he said aloud to himself. He sat back in the chair and ran his fingers through his sandy colored hair. 'Maybe I shouldn't have shown her,' he thought.

"Ethan? What's wrong?" said Louise as she walked up to him. "You look upset, like you've seen a ghost."

"I… I don't know what just happened," he said. "I think Anna just broke up with me."

"That can't be possible, dear," she said.

"She was quite clear. But then again, she wasn't. She sounded so confused, and I don't know what to think."

"Well, did she say why?" asked Louise.

"She said she couldn't live like this, that I was making her keep things from her friends and family, which I'm not. I would never keep her from being honest with the people she loves. But she didn't give me a chance to tell her that. Louise, I just don't know what's going on," Ethan said, leaning forward now in his chair with his hands on his face.

"My dear Ethan," said Louise. "It seems like you two are miscommunicating."

"You're probably right, but I don't know how to change that."

"That's because this is the first young woman you've felt this way about before. When we communicate with our emotions, sometimes we think the other knows exactly what the other is thinking, but that's just not always the case." Louise settled down in a nearby chair, the dreamy look of recalling fond memories flushed over her face. "My Jeffery and I, in the beginning, we always thought that a special look, a kiss, and a touch were enough to convey how we felt. But really, it's so easy when emotions are high to skip past the hard work of really talking to one another."

"That makes sense," said Ethan.

"Of course it does," Louise laughed. "Eventually, Jeffery and I learned that the talking, the communicating, was one of the most important aspects of our relationship, so we learned to make the time for it every day."

"I thought we were talking," Ethan said. "We said so much about what we wanted in life, our dreams, our thoughts."

"Yes, all that is important," Louise continued. "But it's those little things where you need to do the most work to really communicate. It's so easy to misunderstand, and so very hard to be upfront about your feelings. You, my dearest Ethan, have always been suspicious of other people's motives, which is why we have all this," she said, waving her hands around to indicate the mansion. "But not giving yourself fully to Anna has left her with the feeling that there is something missing. I don't know the dear girl well enough, but I suspect she's had people in her past who have let her down. She doesn't want that to ever happen to her again."

"I can understand that. I just wish she'd tell me about that," he said.

"Well, I remember you told me that some young man had practically accosted you all at the county fair. Did you ever ask her about him?" asked Louise.

"No, I didn't want to pry," he answered.

"It's not prying to ask what that man did to her so that you understand her life and her feelings. Her experience with him has shaped her, and it's something you'll need to always know in the future."

"If we have a future," Ethan said. "I love this woman, Louise. I don't know how my life will be if I don't have a future with her."

"You will, my dear," said Louise. "You and Anna will have a wonderful future."

CHAPTER TWENTY

Anna had cried nearly all night, finally passing out from exhaustion.

It was nearly noon when she woke up the next day to hear her phone ringing. 'Thank goodness it's summer vacation,' she thought.

Groggy, she reached over to grab her phone, noticing the number of the caller. "Just what I don't need," she said aloud to herself, but she answered anyway.

"Hello?"

"Hi Anna." It was Alan, and he had a strange tone of voice. "Did you give any thought to our date?"

"Date?" said Anna, still half awake and not yet ready for the conversation.

"Yes, Anna," Alan said impatiently. "I asked you out on a date, and I've been waiting well over twenty-four hours for an answer."

"Alan, I'm sorry, but I'm just not ready for that."

"Not ready!?" Alan half screamed, "You've had plenty of time to think about it."

The controlling, impatient Alan she had known before had reappeared in an instant. Anna hesitated, thought for a moment about the techniques she and Kelly had practiced to deal with him, and adjusted her voice to be assertive and firm.

"I do have an answer, Alan. And that answer is no, thank you. We won't be dating."

Alan exploded. "Oh, is that how you're gonna be, then? You promised me a date and here you go again, lying and sneaking around and getting all miss prissy about everything."

Anna felt her hands shaking, that same old involuntary response she'd had in the turbulent final months of their relationship. "I'm not lying or sneaking around, and I don't have to answer to you."

"Well, Miss Anna, I guess you're getting all full of yourself hanging around with Mister Perfect then," Alan snarled.

"Whom I date and what I do is no longer any of your business. This conversation is over. Goodbye," Anna said, and hung up the phone.

She was trembling even harder, but she managed to call Kelly right away.

"Hi Anna," Kelly answered, having seen Anna's number as her phone rang.

"Can you come over?" Anna asked.

"I'll be there in five," Kelly answered, instantly recognizing the terror in Anna's voice. "Do I need to bring John?"

"No, that's okay. He's not here or anything. It was a phone call," Anna answered.

"Phone call? What the … Ugh, I'll be right there. Keep your doors locked," Kelly instructed.

* * *

KELLY ARRIVED SO QUICKLY THAT ANNA DIDN'T HAVE TIME TO CHANGE out of her nightgown. She got up and let her in, locking the door behind her.

"What did that asshole do now?" Kelly asked her after the friends hugged.

"He called, asking for a date. I told him no and he freaked out," Anna explained.

"A date? Why on earth would that bastard call you? Why would you answer?" Kelly was angry, but she switched her tone when she noticed tears welling up in Anna's eyes. "Oh, Anna, I'm sorry. I'm mad at him, not you. You didn't do anything wrong."

"I know. It's just that same old Alan," said Anna, fighting back tears.

"That jerk will never change. You need to block his number, and if he keeps coming around here, get a restraining order," suggested Kelly.

"Yeah, I guess. I don't know if I can do that though."

"You most certainly can. Remember, he has put his hands on you before," Kelly reminded her. Anna didn't need reminding. That day was still crystal clear in her mind. Everything had started out well as Anna and Alan went shopping together, but then he imagined that she'd been flirting with a cashier in one of the stores. His demeanor turned cold and evil, and got worse when they got home and were alone together. Anna hadn't flirted with anyone, and she told Alan that. But he just got angrier, and he grabbed her--the whole incident was too horrible to remember.

"I remember," Anna whispered.

"It'll be alright. I can stay here tonight, and he'll be over it by tomorrow," suggested Kelly. "He's probably been drinking today, and he'll sober up."

Anna managed a smile for her friend. "Thank you, Kelly. I can always count on you."

"Yes. Yes, you can," Kelly said. "Now, we also need to talk about Ethan. Forget about that Alan moron. Have you eaten?" Kelly made her way to Anna's kitchen before she had a chance to answer, every bit as comfortable in Anna's home as her own. Anna followed her.

"I was up late last night, so I just got up," said Anna. "And I broke up with Ethan last night."

"What? Why?" Kelly was reaching for some cereal and stopped in her tracks. "Did something happen?"

"Not really," Anna said, unhappy that she couldn't tell her friend about the mansion and all she'd experienced. "I just remembered how things seemed great with Alan in the beginning and then look what happened. Things seem great with Ethan now, but…"

"Oh, my friend, my beautiful, silly friend. Ethan is NOT Alan. They're like not even from the same planet. I don't think they even get to breathe the same quality of oxygen on THIS planet. There's like, some sort of filter that gives the good stuff to that Greek god of a man Ethan," Kelly laughed.

Anna laughed, too. "I needed the laugh," she said. "I know, they are definitely not the same."

"No. And honey, I love you and you're my best friend, so I'm going to be straight with you. You just can't keep letting the bad people in this world hold you back from what's good for you. And Ethan IS good for you. I know it in my heart," said Kelly.

"I know, but there are things you don't know about him…"

"If you told me he just spontaneously grew a third arm, I would still say he's good for you," said Kelly. "Remember, we spent all night at the fair together. He's amazing. He's a caring man and a gentleman."

"Yeah, I know. You're right, Kelly."

"So what's probably happening is lots of miscommunication. You need to talk to the man, Anna. Tell him what you've gone through and why you feel afraid to start a relationship. I know that he'll make you feel better about it. You need to talk about these things so he understands, and I know he will. But he can't read your mind," Kelly said.

"Yes, you're right again."

"I know I am," Kelly laughed. "And you need to go see the man. But first, let's eat," she laughed again.

Anna smiled. "Okay, I'll go over there today."

CHAPTER TWENTY-ONE

After Kelly and Anna ate, Kelly encouraged her to get dressed and head over to Ethan's house to clear the air.

"This kind of conversation is best done in person. You need to go see him," Kelly had advised.

As soon as she was dressed and ready, she got in her car and pulled out of her driveway. Kelly waved to her from Anna's porch, smiling. She stayed behind to make sure everything was locked up securely, since Anna had been through such an emotional time lately and might forget something. Kelly worried for her friend's safety after hearing how Alan had been acting.

* * *

Anna pulled up to the farmhouse, parked her car, and headed up to the door. She had a whole new perspective on the small, charming home knowing what was hidden underneath.

Her knock on the door went unanswered, and she assumed Ethan was downstairs and would take some time to answer, so she wandered around back into his garden.

The view was stunning, as the garden was situated in the bright sun on top of a large hill. It overlooked a rolling countryside, where different shades of green delineated the various fields of crops. Anna could see for miles. She walked over to a small flower garden several yards away and sat on a wooden bench in the shade of a giant tree. Not long after, a tabby cat walked up and jumped into her lap.

"Well, hello there," Anna said. "Milo, right?"

"That's right," said Ethan, who had walked up behind her. "I'm so sorry I kept you waiting. It takes a while to walk from the lounge to the elevator on this side of the property."

"That's okay," Anna said with a smile. "I need to talk to you."

"All good things, I hope," said Ethan as he sat down beside her. Milo moved to sit between them and Ethan scratched him under his chin.

"I think so. I've had time to think. Sometimes I think too much, and maybe that's been the problem here. I think we've miscommunicated," Anna said.

Ethan slid his hand over on top of Anna's and squeezed gently. "I agree. I didn't take the time to understand how much you'd been hurt before."

"It's hard to talk about. So many bad memories come out when I do think about Alan, that I think it's my fault for holding it all in."

"It's not your fault, Anna."

"I think it is, in a way. No, it's not my fault what Alan did to me before, but I should have talked to you about how much that made me shy away from our relationship instead of just cutting you off like that," she said, looking straight into his sky-blue eyes.

"Tell me now," Ethan said as he brought his other hand to hers.

"He… he was abusive. Physically a little, but mostly he had me in a kind of emotional stranglehold, and I just couldn't let go. It was a terrible way to live, and it tore me up inside."

"I'm so sorry you had to go through that," said Ethan.

"It's not your fault, and it has nothing to do with you, but what happened is I remembered how things started with Alan. It was really wonderful in the beginning. With the way things are also so wonderful with us now, I was afraid," explained Anna.

"That's perfectly natural," Ethan said in a comforting voice. "Having a relationship like that will have lasting effects."

"Yes, and it was so subtle that I didn't even notice how it affected me - until it affected you ... affected us." She looked into his eyes again. "I'm so sorry, Ethan."

He gave a light, gentle laugh that told Anna everything would be okay. "You have nothing to apologize for. We haven't had enough time to talk about things as intense as how the past has affected us. That will be part of our lives going forward as our relationship builds. And I know that takes time, Anna, which is why I told you that we can go as slow as you need to."

"Well, I also worried because I can't talk to Kelly or my parents about this place, or what's going on with you, and that really bothers me," said Anna.

"Sweetheart, I never said you couldn't tell the people you love about this place, or about me, or about anything else you want to talk about with them," said Ethan.

"I can? Well, I guess I just assumed that you'd want to keep it quiet."

He laughed gently again. "I think we both assumed things without talking them over first," he said.

"I guess we did," she agreed.

"Let's make a pact that we'll try not to ever assume anything again. If we're not sure about something, we'll talk about it," he suggested.

"That sounds wonderful," she agreed. "How should we make a pact?"

"Well, I think the best way is to seal the agreement with a kiss," he said.

She smiled, scooting closer to him. "I can't think of a nicer way to make an agreement."

He smiled and moved in, and they gazed into each other's eyes for a moment before their lips met. They melted into the kiss together, each feeling the magnetic pull of attraction as well as the pleasure of pure emotion as the weight of uncertainty lifted away.

"I'm falling in love with you, Anna," he said as they parted.

"And I'm falling in love with you, too, Ethan," she said, "And I'll try not to be afraid of those feelings anymore."

"It's okay to be afraid, Anna," he told her. "Just when you feel fear, tell me about it, and we'll talk it through."

"I will," she promised, smiling as they held hands.

"I do have a lot more to show you, if you have the time," he said.

"Yes, I'd love to see!" she exclaimed.

They rose, walking back to the farmhouse. Along the way, Anna quickly texted Kelly to let her know that everything was going well. Then they traveled down the elevator to explore more of the incredible underground mansion.

CHAPTER TWENTY-TWO

THE ELEVATOR DESCENDED, and Ethan showed Anna to a part of the mansion she had not yet seen.

"This is the heart and soul of everything we do here, and it's why this place exists," he said as they neared a door at the end of the hallway.

The door slid open as they approached, revealing a huge room full of people and high-tech equipment. The room buzzed with the sound of computers, printers, and other equipment Anna didn't recognize, as well as the sounds of the team members talking. The bustle of activity paused when Anna and Ethan entered the room, and the team turned to them, smiling.

"This is the team, Anna," explained Ethan. "Team, this is Anna." She was welcomed with 'hellos' and 'how are yous' coming from all sides of the room.

"Hello, everyone," Anna said, smiling. "I'm happy to meet you all."

"You'll meet everyone on a more one-on-one basis later, but for now, let me show you a few things," Ethan explained.

"What is it all these people do here?" Anna asked.

"This is our communication and research hub. In addition to the work we do for my corporation back in LA, we do two more things here. We do research and vet different charities, initiatives, and people so we can choose where we can do the most good. We also keep in constant communication with important suppliers and contacts that help us on our mission," Ethan explained.

"Charities?" Anna asked.

"Yes, our mission here, and the reason this whole place exists," he said, waving his hand to indicate the underground facilities, "is to use our funds for charities and for helping people in the best way we can. I didn't want to just throw money at people and then leave them hanging when that ran out. I wanted to be a part of building a better future, and that takes a huge commitment. I didn't just build a mansion to have a fancy place to live. I built it for these people, my team," he said as he smiled at everyone, who had mostly gone back to being busy on computers or meeting on the room's many tables.

"That's amazing," Anna said.

"Everyone here is a trusted member of my team. Most have been with me for years, some not as long, but all are equally committed to the team's mission. We all take shifts here, and everyone stays in a private room for their shifts. Some bring their families here. Others come for shorter shifts and then go home to their families," Ethan explained. "When they're here doing the important work we do, I want everyone to be comfortable."

"I'm definitely impressed," Anna said. "What kinds of charitable things do you do?" she asked. In that moment, she understood even more how different Ethan was from Alan. Alan had always done things for himself. Even when he had extra money, he always saved it for something he wanted to buy. Sometimes she had asked him to help out with a needy student in her class, but he would never even buy a child a backpack or other supplies. Alan had no room in his heart for charities. For Ethan, doing good for the world was clearly a priority.

"Lots of different things. Here, let's go see what Cliff's team is working with as an example," Ethan suggested. They walked over to a nearby table where a shorter man and a team of men and women were looking over some papers and talking to someone via teleconference on a screen in the center of the table.

"Hi Ethan," said the man. Everyone else nodded and smiled at Anna as they approached.

"Hey, Cliff," answered Ethan. "What's the team working on here?"

"Our project is a unique start-up school in a very rural area in South America," Cliff explained. "There are a few logistical issues to work out to get it developed, so we're brainstorming how to make that happen. We have our local folks on conference here, explaining the challenges."

Anna was instantly interested, being a schoolteacher herself. "I'm a teacher. Is there some way I can help?" she asked.

"Oh, absolutely. We're always looking for expertise," said Cliff.

Ethan pulled up a couple of chairs so they could sit and join the conversation. They spent the next hour and a half as part of the team, working on plans for development of the school and its community, as well as ideas for curriculum that would engage the kids while teaching skills that would enhance the community in the future.

"It's amazing how many details go into planning a project like this," said Anna after working with the team.

"Absolutely," agreed Ethan. "That's why you can't just throw money at a challenge. You have to stick around, work out the details, and help make the project successful, or it won't truly help anyone."

They wrapped up the meeting, and everyone was assigned tasks to complete before they'd meet again the next week.

Anna went with Cliff to his workstation so they could do some more work on curriculum plans. Ethan joined other groups to become part of their discussions as the day went on. Anna would look over at Ethan every so often. His eyes were bright and alert, his conversations were animated and excited, and he seemed to be completely energized by the entire endeavor. She smiled, thrilled at what a good soul he was, full of genuine compassion and high moral standards. He thought about others before himself.

It was a busy day, and eventually everyone started to clear up their workstations and finish up their projects for the day. Ethan walked up to Anna.

"It's been a long day. Will you join me for dinner, Anna?" he asked.

"Of course," she smiled, taking the hand he had offered her to guide her out of the control room area.

"I'll see you later, Cliff," she said.

"See you tomorrow, Anna," Cliff answered. "Thanks for all your help today. It was amazing."

"Thanks," she said with a smile, and she and Ethan walked out of the room. "What's for dinner?" she asked Ethan as they strolled down the hallway.

"It's always a surprise," he said, "but Chef Benjamin never disappoints."

"I'm sure it'll be delicious," she said, smiling as they headed toward the dining room.

CHAPTER TWENTY-THREE

Chef Benjamin had prepared a special dinner to welcome Anna back, and the whole team was excited to see Anna and Ethan back together. The team members were close friends of Ethan, and they had watched him care for so many others over the years while never taking care of his own needs, so they were excited to see him finding love. They had never seen him this way, with a measurable spring in his step and a sparkle in his eyes that told the world that he had finally found the one woman for him.

For Anna, all those feelings of uncertainty had washed away when she discovered the true reason behind Ethan's secret underground mansion, that it was a place for a team of dedicated people - with Ethan at the helm - who worked quietly to make the world a better place. None of them asked for recognition. They did it with a sense of duty and responsibility, and the team was a true reflection of its leader, Ethan.

"This is amazing," said Anna.

"I'm glad you like it. Benjamin is truly a genius," Ethan added.

"It's not just the food, which yes, it's all truly amazing. But it's that something has happened to me tonight," Anna explained.

"Happened?"

"I don't really know how to put it. But yes, something has changed. My past - it finally feels like a past. It's all a haze, almost like something that happened to someone else. There's this huge weight that's lifted and my future is so much clearer now," she said.

"Why do you think that happened so suddenly?" he asked. "I mean, I couldn't be happier, but it wasn't long ago that you were so uncertain."

"It's you, it's coming back to you and being with you again. But it's also me. I was energized in that room. I felt like I had an over-whelming purpose," she explained. "Like everything I've ever dreamed about for my future of helping others is within my reach now."

"That's exactly how I feel," Ethan agreed. "It's why I do what I do. I knew it would have the same effect on you. I just felt it. We were meant to be together."

Anna smiled, "I'm so happy," she said.

"So am I," Ethan agreed. "Shall we take a walk?"

"Absolutely."

Ethan started to gather the dishes, but Louise appeared, seemingly from nowhere, and insisted they go enjoy themselves. "This is a night for the two of you. Have fun," she told them.

"Well, I think we've been commanded to leave," Ethan laughed.

"Let's go," said Anna, and they strolled down the hallways, Ethan showing her all the artwork and other details that she hadn't seen before.

* * *

OUTSIDE, A CAR PULLED OVER, JUST OFF THE ROAD NEAR THE ENTRANCE to Ethan's farmland. Its headlights dimmed.

* * *

HOLDING HANDS, ETHAN AND ANNA CAME TO A ROOM AT THE END OF A long hallway.

"This is my room," Ethan told her. He looked knowingly into her eyes. "Would you like to see it?"

She smiled and squeezed his hand. "Yes," she whispered.

The large suite was decorated primarily in red and black, with a sitting area furnished with a couch, chair, and cherry wood table, with a giant screen flush against the nearby wall. Behind the sitting area was Ethan's large bed with an intricately carved wooden headboard.

He turned to her and took her in his arms. She met him halfway, and their lips joined together as if they had been starving for each other for years. They parted for a moment and he led her over to the bed, where they both sat down and instantly resumed the kiss.

"Are you sure?" Ethan asked between kisses. "You wanted to go slow."

"Not anymore," she said, breathlessly.

After a few minutes, he turned her and laid her down on the bed with her legs still over the side. "I want you," he told her.

"I want you, too."

He got up and walked around the bed, removing his shirt and lying on the pillows, pulling her gently up the bed toward him. They kissed more, and he showered her neck with delicate kisses, reaching down to lift off her shirt. She helped, taking off her shirt and bra as he reached to undo her pants. He slid them off, leaving her in only her panties. He wrapped his arms around her, holding her tighter than she'd ever been held before as they felt each other's heartbeats. Time stood still as they held each other for that moment, then they both finished undressing and melted into each other, each simultaneously giving and receiving pleasure for hours, until their hearts and bodies were fully satiated.

They collapsed beside each other, out of breath, their fingers still interlocked.

Ethan turned his head and looked deep into her emerald eyes. "I can't believe I finally found you," he told her. "I love you, Anna."

"I love you too, Ethan," she said.

* * *

RICK

SEVERAL HALLWAYS AWAY FROM THE LIVING QUARTERS, RICK WAS finishing up his shift in the security room. The farmland was always quiet, but they still maintained some fairly sophisticated security measures to protect the property. The security room was small compared to some of the other rooms, filled with screens displaying video from the many cameras outside and inside the property. An alarm sounded on one of the monitors, and Rick quickly turned his attention to the screen.

"Hmm," he said. "That's weird." It was rare that anything appeared on a screen other than wild animals. Another man, who was about to take over for the night shift, moved over to watch the screen. "Who is that?" he asked.

"I have no idea, Jim," Rick admitted. "But I'm going to find out."

"Looks like he's coming near the barn," said Jim. The entrance to the underground parking garage was located in an abandoned-looking barn near the front of the property. Located behind a grove of trees, it could not be seen from the road. "He seems like he knows it's there. That's impossible," Jim observed.

"Yeah, I'm going up," Rick said.

"I'm going with you."

The men grabbed their jackets, flashlights, and their weapons and headed to the parking garage. They were both trained in firearms and kept them on the property, but neither had ever had a need to fire a gun in or around the underground mansion.

The entrance to the garage was no ordinary barn, but none of that could be seen from the outside. Each of the team members had a special remote control that opened the barn for cars to drive in. Once inside, there was a ramp leading to a large sliding warehouse door that opened into the parking area below. A separate elevator was nearby for foot traffic, and this is where Rick and Jim emerged to investigate the intruder.

Alan Shangle had been examining the tire tracks near the barn when he heard noises and voices inside. He started to run. The men gave chase, but Alan was already back in his car and quickly drove away. They made a note of his license plate number, since neither man had recognized Alan.

* * *

DOWN IN ETHAN'S SUITE, ANNA AND ETHAN FELL ASLEEP IN EACH other's arms with carefree smiles on their faces as they snuggled safely together.

CHAPTER TWENTY-FOUR

THE NEXT MORNING, Anna and Ethan awoke still holding one another.

"Good morning," Ethan said as he reached over to kiss her.

"Good morning," she answered, and their lips met with a warm familiarity.

"I could get used to this," he said, smiling.

"And you will," she said playfully.

Feeling relaxed and comfortable, they fell back into each other's arms and made love once again.

"I could do this all day," Ethan laughed when they finished.

"Oh, no," Anna said, suddenly sitting up in bed.

"What, you don't want me to?" Ethan said, laughing lightheartedly.

"No, I mean yes, but it's not that. I forgot. I mean, I just realized I promised the school's principal that I'd help out with classes today. A few of their summer school teachers are on an overnight field trip and won't be back." She looked over at Ethan. "I'm so sorry. I think I have to leave. I don't want to go."

"It's okay, Anna. We have plenty of time for nights like this," said Ethan. "Good thing we woke up early."

"Yes, I have plenty of time, but I need to go home first and get ready. I'm so sorry," she said again, kissing him.

"Anna," he laughed, "you don't have to be sorry that you have responsibilities. I have them, too. We'll enjoy being together later on."

They both got dressed and Ethan walked Anna out to her car.

"Are you sure you don't have time for breakfast?" he asked. "We could make something quick."

"It was so silly of me to forget. I'll just grab something from home and eat it at my desk. It's only a half day class."

They said their goodbyes and kissed several times before Anna got in her car and left.

* * *

BACK DOWNSTAIRS, RICK APPROACHED ETHAN AS HE WAS HEADED TO the dining room.

"There was someone outside snooping around last night," Rick told him.

"What? Who on earth would do that?"

"We got the license plate, and I was able to find out a name through my contacts. Alan Shangle is the registered owner. Ring a bell?" asked Rick.

"Oh, no. I have to tell Anna," Ethan said, getting out his phone and texting her. "Did he see anything?"

"No, he was snooping outside the barn but never got inside."

"Okay, that's good then," said Ethan.

"I'll beef up security so he doesn't get that close again."

"Thanks, Rick."

Anna didn't answer his text right away because she was still headed home. He desperately wanted to call her to warn her, but he didn't want to distract her while driving, so he waited to hear from her.

* * *

ANNA HEARD THE TEXT AS SHE DROVE DOWN THE ROAD, BUT DIDN'T check it to look until she was in her driveway. She called Ethan when she arrived home.

"What's wrong?" she asked.

"It's Alan. I don't want to scare you, but he was snooping around the property here last night."

"What?! Alan …"

"Yes. Are you alright there?"

"Yes, everything is fine," she said. "Stay on the phone with me while I go inside."

Nothing seemed out of place and the doors were all still locked, so Anna told Ethan that everything was fine. "I can't let him run my life."

"No, but please be careful."

"I will. I'll be back over later tonight."

"Okay, sweetheart. Have a good day in class."

"I will," she said. "I love you."

"I love you, too, Anna."

Anna was slightly upset at the news about Alan, but like she had told Ethan the night before, everything about Alan seemed like a distant past, like she hadn't even lived through it. Quickly she moved on and enjoyed her day with a new sense of happiness. Her future was as bright and cheerful as this summer day, and nothing could interfere with her good mood.

After work, she pulled into her driveway and into the back just in front of her garage. She would leave later for Ethan's house, so she kept her car out of the garage and started to step outside. She had barely stood up when Alan came up behind her, his voice hoarse and cold and his demeanor shaking and angry. He smelled of alcohol.

"You slut," he hollered at her, "you're supposed to be my wife, and there you are cheating on me!"

Anna fought to maintain her composure. "I'm not your wife, and I never was."

"Well, you're my fiancé, at least. You promised to marry me and that's what you're gonna do."

"No, I am not," she insisted.

"Feeling like little Miss Priss 'cause you're messing with Mr. Wonderful out there in the country? Well, I know he's up to something illegal and I'm gonna find out what! Then you'll come back to me."

"What are you talking about?"

"He's got people coming and going and it's gotta be something illegal and I'm gonna know what," said Alan, his speech starting to slur. "And I'm gonna tell the whole town about him. The whole state, the whole …"

"You need to leave, Alan."

"I'm going nowhere till you marry me like you said," insisted Alan, stumbling over the words so they were barely coherent.

Anna knew this tone of voice all too well, and there was no reasoning with Alan in this condition. The best thing to do was to play along just to get rid of him. She couldn't reach her phone and didn't have her keys in her hand, so she had nothing nearby to use as a weapon if he got violent.

"Fine," she lied, "I'll think about it, but you have to give me time, so I need you to go home right now."

"Uh, okay but I'll remember that you said that because you said that before…." His words trailed off, no longer making any sense. He looked like he would fall over any moment, so Anna took the opportunity to grab her keys and phone, then she slipped by him and made her way into her house, locking the door behind her.

Her first call was to Ethan.

CHAPTER TWENTY-FIVE

"He was here," Anna told Ethan when he answered the phone. He instantly knew who the "he" was.

"What?! I can be there in five minutes," Ethan said, panicking and running toward the parking garage.

"I'm okay. It's okay. He wandered off and he's not here anymore. I'm locked inside."

He slowed to a walk. "I can still come over and make sure he stays away. Or you can come over here, where I can protect you."

"I'll be over later for dinner, but I'm not going to let Alan Shangle run me out of my own home. I've worked too hard for everything I have."

"I can respect that. I'm just worried about you. Will you let me at least send some security people over to keep an eye on things? No one will even know they're around, but they'll confront him if he comes back," suggested Ethan.

"Okay. That would actually make me feel better. I don't want him doing anything to my house, or to Sammy."

"It's as good as done. I'll have a team assembled, and they'll be there in ten minutes. I'll keep them there until we deal with this lunatic once and for all."

"Well, I'm not sure how we're going to do that. He drinks, and he just gets stupid," Anna explained.

"We'll figure it out. In the meantime, my people are well trained to handle people like that."

"I feel better already, Ethan. I love you."

"I love you, too, Anna. Which is why I worry," he said before changing the subject. "What time are you coming to dinner? I'll have Chef Benjamin make one of his specialties."

"That would be wonderful! But I have an idea. I know you wanted just the two of us, but would it be okay if Kelly joined us, and we brought her up to speed on everything?"

"Of course," Ethan said with a smile that Anna could feel, even though he wasn't in the room with her. "Bring her boyfriend, too. What is his name?"

"John," said Anna.

"Yes, John. Nice guy. I trust him, too, to know our secret."

"I'll have to call and ask them, but I'm sure they'll say yes. I'll let you know."

"I'll talk to you soon then. Please be careful, Anna. I'll have my people there soon," he said.

"I will. I'll call you right back and let you know."

As he was talking on the phone, Ethan was heading toward the security room so he could assemble a team to watch over Anna's house. He quickly briefed Rick on the situation.

"We'll be there in five," Rick said.

"Thanks, Rick," Ethan said.

Anna, meanwhile, was calling Kelly.

"Girl, what took you so long to call me?" demanded Kelly as soon as she answered. "No, never mind, no news means you were, um, busy," she added with a giggle.

"Actually, we were," Anna laughed.

"I knew it!" Kelly exclaimed.

"Now, don't start with that," Anna said. "I've called to invite you both on another double date. Do you guys have plans tonight?"

"We do now," Kelly answered. "Where are we headed?"

"Out to Ethan's house for dinner."

"Oh, he doesn't have to go through all that trouble."

"Trust me, it's no trouble," Anna said. "You'll understand that more later," she added with a laugh.

"Okayyy," said Kelly, stretching out the word.

"So what time? Anything works for us," Anna said.

"How about we meet you there at seven?" Kelly asked.

"Perfect. You know where it is, right?"

"Everyone in town knows where that gorgeous hunk of a man lives," laughed Kelly.

"Okay," Anna chuckled. "I'll see you then!"

They said their goodbyes and hung up around the same time that Anna noticed a couple of black SUVs drive by. 'Well, that's not very discreet,' she thought to herself, 'but I feel safer now.' She watched Ethan's team park near the back of the nearby church but didn't see where they went.

"Well, he's right. No one will see them now," she said aloud.

She finally had a moment to herself to digest what had happened earlier. Any remnant of her feelings for Alan had now completely disappeared, and the thought amazed her. The fear that had enveloped her so strongly over the past years seemed like just a bad dream.

"This is like a dream," she said aloud to herself, and Sammy looked up at her.

As with a dream, she felt that rush of relief one has when awakening and realizing that nothing in that dream can hurt them anymore. Although Alan was still physically present in the real world, she felt the power of the all-encompassing protection of Ethan and his expansive team, knowing that anything a jerk like Alan could think up would be swiftly dealt with by the team.

How had she ever felt anything for such a man? Was it that she had no other good men in her life by which to compare? It couldn't be, because she had John, a strong and protective friend, and her father, always caring and understanding, not to mention many more of her male friends and coworkers with good-natured personalities, so plenty of good men had been in her life even before Ethan. She shook her head, chalking it all up to her youth and inexperience. From now on, she resolved never to be so naïve again.

Looking at the clock, she noticed that she had a few hours before dinner and decided to treat herself to a nice, warm bath. Running the water and watching the bubbles foam up, she felt safe knowing that Ethan's ever-present and loving protection was right outside.

CHAPTER TWENTY-SIX

After her relaxing bath, Anna changed and left for Ethan's house a little early so that she'd be there when Kelly and John arrived. Before leaving, she let one of Ethan's security team members, Linda, into her house so she could monitor things while Anna was gone.

"Make yourself at home, Linda," Anna said. "There's plenty to eat and drink in the kitchen, so help yourself. I really appreciate you helping me out."

"Anytime. My husband, Rick, and I have known Ethan for years. They're best friends, and we're all so happy to see Ethan finally find the right woman," said Linda.

"Thank you. You're all such wonderful friends," said Anna.

Anna headed over to Ethan's and arrived shortly before her friends.

"I'm so excited to show them!" she told Ethan. "They're both going to be shocked."

"That does seem to be the general first reaction," laughed Ethan.

When Kelly and John arrived, Anna and Ethan were waiting for them in the driveway in front of the farmhouse.

"Oh, this is such an adorable place!" exclaimed Kelly as she gave her friend a quick hug. The men gave each other a friendly hand-shake, then Anna hugged John as well.

"I'm so excited that you two are here," she said. "I can't wait to show you everything."

John and Kelly looked a bit confused as Anna quickly led them past the main rooms of the farmhouse they'd expected to tour, walking straight to the elevator room. "Hold on," she said as the elevator descended.

The elevator opened to the hallway with the raining water fountain, and both Kelly and John were wide-eyed with amazement.

"Let's show them the communications room first," Anna suggested to Ethan. "That one really answered most of my questions right away."

"Good idea," Ethan said as he led the group down the hallways. As they walked, there were plenty of "oohs" and "ahhs" to be heard as John and Kelly took in the sights of the amazing underground mansion.

When they entered the communication center, it wasn't quite as impressive as Anna had first seen it, since almost all of the team had wrapped up work for the day. Cliff and his team were still hard at work, however, and they were happy to give Kelly and John a quick rundown of the project.

Anna, Ethan, Kelly, and John then went over to their own confer-ence table so Ethan could explain things further. He told them about the mission, how the mansion was built and why, and all about the team. Of course, Kelly and John were more than impressed.

"This is just so … unbelievable," said Kelly. "It's all so wonderfully overwhelming."

"I agree," said John. "And now I feel completely and totally useless as a human being."

Kelly laughed, and the rest joined in. "You're a big goof," she said.

A tone sounded on Ethan's cell phone, and he checked his text messages. "Looks like our dinner is ready, folks. Come along this way," he said as he led them to the dining room.

The table was set with beautiful antique dishes with sterling silverware and beautiful forest green linens. A candelabra in the center lit the room with a romantic glow.

Soon after they were seated, Louise and some other team members brought drinks and appetizers to the table, and the two couples enjoyed a lively conversation about the mansion, their first double date at the county fair, and John's talent for fixing cars.

"We could certainly use a mechanic, if you'd like a side job, or even a new full-time job," Ethan said.

"Wow, that would be incredible, thanks," John said. "I'd want to be hired for my talent, not because I'm a friend of Anna's, though."

"Of course," said Ethan. "We hire everyone here on merits, but they do also happen to be friends. It's a bit of a necessity here, since everyone has to be onboard for the mission and willing to keep this place under wraps," he explained. "No one really does just one thing here - unless there's just one thing that they're passionate about. We all just sort of jump in where things are needed, and eventually, we really get to know our own strengths and find the tasks that fit."

"That makes sense," John said.

Eventually, everyone finished Chef Benjamin's incredible dinner, including an amazing dessert of homemade pies and ice cream, and Ethan suggested they head to the lounge for drinks.

"Wow, you have your own private dance club here," John said, looking around in awe.

"Yes, the team deserves to relax, so we make pretty good use of this room," Ethan explained.

"Is there a lady's room nearby?" Kelly asked.

"I'll show you," said Anna, leading her down the hall. When they were out of earshot of the men, Kelly said, "You are the luckiest woman on this planet, Anna Shelby."

"I know," said Anna, "and I couldn't be happier."

"I'm so happy for you," said Kelly. "You're positively glowing with joy. I never thought I'd see this day, but I certainly prayed for it over the years."

"Thank you, Kelly," said Anna. "You're the best friend ever."

"So are you," Kelly said with a smile.

When they returned to the lounge, the men were relaxing with drinks.

"What'll you have?" asked Ethan, playing the bartender.

"I'm afraid I'm going to have to stick with a soda," said Anna. "They've asked me to help out another day in summer school tomorrow, so I'll have to get up early."

"Looks like we're mostly going with non-alcoholic drinks tonight," said Ethan. "I didn't get a chance to tell you this earlier, sweetheart, but I'm going to have to run to LA for a day or so tomorrow. There's a big business deal happening for my company, and I have to be there to sign papers and meet the client in person. I was hoping you could come along."

"I'd love to see your hometown, but I made this promise to the kids to be there, and I just can't let them down," said Anna.

"It's okay," said Ethan. "We'll plan a leisure trip to LA some other time when we'll have more time to relax. In the meantime, I'd like to propose a toast - to wonderful friendships!"

Everyone raised their glasses in a toast, and they spent a couple of hours exchanging stories, laughing, and talking about the past and the future. Eventually, the conversation turned to Alan.

"Oh, just give me five minutes, and I'll handle that Alan Shangle," said John.

"He wouldn't stick around near you for five minutes to give you the chance," Kelly laughed. "He's terrified of you."

"He should be," said John. "It'll only take one swing…"

"You are not going to jail for beating up that loser," said Kelly. "He's not worth it."

"I have security watching Anna's place, and I think I have a plan for dealing with him without getting anyone in trouble," said Ethan. "He doesn't know who he's dealing with, and that's an advantage."

"I will leave it to the experts, then, and stick with pillow fights with Kelly, here," said John. "I always win."

"You always lose, you big dork," said Kelly, and the group laughed.

It started to get late, so eventually Kelly and John headed home. Ethan walked Anna out to her car.

"I'll miss you while you're gone," she said.

"I'll be back just as soon as I can. And while I'm gone, security will be watching both your place and Kelly's. I don't want anything to happen to your friends, either."

"Thank you," she said. "I love you so much."

"I love you, too, my beautiful Anna," he said as their lips met for a lingering kiss. Many moments later they parted, and Anna got in her car to drive home.

* * *

ALAN SHANGLE'S LIGHT BLUE SEDAN DROVE BY ANNA'S HOUSE AND slowed down. Observing a woman's figure in the light behind the curtains, he assumed Anna was home alone for the night and drove on. Another security guard, watching from his car in the shadows of the nearby church parking lot, made a note of the time on a chart.

Shortly after, Anna safely pulled into her driveway.

CHAPTER TWENTY-SEVEN

ANNA AWOKE EARLY the next day as the sun streaked in between her bedroom curtains. Half-awake, she gave Sammy a quick pet and laid still for a while, thinking about her relationship with Ethan. Would she move into the mansion with him? If he asked, she could hardly pass up the opportunity. But looking at all the little decorative touches she'd acquired with so much care, she wondered how she could leave the little home she'd worked so hard for.

She had promised that she'd help at the school for one more day, so she put her thoughts about the future aside for now and ate breakfast, got dressed, and headed to the school.

Finished with their day, Anna and Kelly left the school and headed over to Kelly's house for dinner. Ethan was out of town on his business trip, but he had texted Anna often, showing pictures of some of the sights around Los Angeles.

"I'd love to visit there," she told him in one of her texts, and he agreed to plan a trip when they both had some time.

Anna loved having time to spend with Kelly, and now they had so much to talk about. John was at Ethan's house getting familiar with what would be his new job as a mechanic there, so the women had some girls-only time to talk. They were in Kelly's kitchen, chopping up vegetables for a stir-fry meal, which was one of Kelly's favorites.

"I'm still in shock," Kelly said. "It's like it's all not even real, but I've seen it with my own eyes," she said, referencing the underground mansion.

"I know how you feel," said Anna. "I honestly didn't know what to think about it at first myself."

"How long have you known?"

"Not long," explained Anna. "But it was just long enough to give me more reasons to be confused about things."

"So that's why you broke up?" Kelly asked with a frown.

"Yes. It added another layer of confusion to everything. I didn't want to have feelings for Ethan because of his money."

"Oh, my dearest friend. You had feelings for that man the moment you laid eyes on him. You haven't been the same since," Kelly laughed. "I swear, you've pretty much had that smile glued to your face ever since you met Ethan Greenfield."

"That's true," Anna agreed with a grin, "but I still wasn't sure. And I couldn't talk to you about it at all."

"Did Ethan actually tell you not to tell me about it?" Kelly asked in disbelief.

"No, he never said that."

"Miscommunicating, again," said Kelly. "I told you that would get you in trouble."

"You're right, of course. I should have listened to you and talked to him more before I made all those assumptions," Anna agreed.

"I'm just glad it's all worked out now," said Kelly. "And that mansion is incredible. I want to see more of it!"

"You will, especially since John is working there now," said Anna. "What did he tell his boss about that, anyway?"

"He didn't," Kelly said with a laugh. "He'll be starting at Ethan's part-time, but that means he'll be working constantly since he's still full-time at the Johnston's." Ted Johnston owned the local auto repair shop where John worked.

"I hope he's not keeping that up very long," said Anna. "You need some time together."

"I know. He knows that, too. He's told Ted that he'll be reducing his hours there. Made up an excuse about helping his parents," Kelly explained. If a person suddenly quit a job in the small town of Belleville, the whole town would start talking, which might eventually raise suspicions about what was happening at Ethan's place.

"That's good. Do they know already?" Anna asked.

"No, we haven't told my parents or his yet, but they never talk to the Johnstons anyway," Kelly laughed. "They think he underpays him, which is true. They'll find out soon, though. Rick told John this morning that all family members of employees know about the mansion."

"That's good to hear. But right now, I'm starving. Let's start cooking!" Anna said.

"Yep, I think we have enough here," agreed Kelly, looking at the supply of chopped vegetables on the counter. She took out the wok and heated up a little sesame oil before adding the vegetables. The food was almost ready when Anna's phone rang.

"Hello?" Anna said to the caller, not recognizing the number.

"Miss Shelby, this is Linda," said the member of Ethan's security team.

"Linda, hi. Please call me Anna. Is everything okay?" Anna asked.

"I'm afraid we found Mr. Spangle hanging around Ms. Skitmore's house, but our guards have scared him away."

"What?" said Anna. "I thought we were done with him." Kelly looked at Anna and mouthed the word, 'Alan' and Anna nodded, returning her attention to the call.

"We have everything under control and continue to keep an eye on both Ms. Skitmore's house and your own, but we wanted you to be aware of the issue. If you plan on going anywhere, please call me at this number first so we can make sure everything is clear outside," Linda advised.

"We will, thank you, Linda. We're not planning on going anywhere tonight, but if we do, we'll let you know first. Thank you so much for helping us," Anna said.

"It's my pleasure. Don't worry, we won't let him anywhere near you."

"Thank you again," repeated Anna.

"What the hell is that moron doing now?" asked Kelly when Anna hung up the phone.

"He was outside somewhere but they scared him away."

"What an idiot," Kelly said, looking around nervously. "I hate to admit it, but he's getting scarier now the way he's been acting."

"I know. And he was at Ethan's," said Anna.

"What?! How did he know to go there?"

"I don't know. He must have followed me or something, but he was there the other night snooping around. Rick and the team scared him off, but now he knows about the place and threatened to tell everyone about it," explained Anna.

"He's seen the mansion?" Kelly asked.

"No, not really, but he's suspicious about the garage entrance, so we have to be careful. That's why I haven't called the police on him."

"Well, there will probably be a point when that's going to have to happen, I'm afraid," said Kelly.

"I know," said Anna, looking down at her phone. She had texted Ethan after the call, and he reassured Anna that she and Kelly were safe, and that the team would take good care of her.

"In the meantime, we're not letting that idiot Alan Shangle ruin this incredible dinner. So let's eat!" Kelly said cheerfully, trying to distract her friend from worry.

"It smells delicious," Anna said as they brought the food to the table. One more text came through on her phone from Ethan as they started eating. He would be home tomorrow.

CHAPTER TWENTY-EIGHT

ETHAN PULLED into the garage entrance after a long, successful business trip back in LA. The clients were happy with the arrangement and were glad to meet Ethan in person, so the deal was signed and development on the project would begin soon.

But Ethan couldn't think about business right now. His only concern was Anna's safety. He knew that Alan had been both physically and emotionally violent in Anna's past, and Ethan worried that things would escalate now that the man knew about Anna's relationship with Ethan. He'd dealt with far too many unstable people in his past business and personal relationships, and he knew how unglued jealous and controlling people could become when the situation became out of their control.

Ethan headed straight to Rick in the security room and found him talking to John.

"John," Ethan said, extending his arm for a handshake, "I'm glad to see you getting started so soon." He and Rick exchanged welcoming nods as Ethan addressed John. "Are Anna and Kelly doing okay?"

"They're fine," John said, "although there was a little scare last night. It shook them up a little, but they know the team is out there watching out for them."

"Good," said Ethan, turning to Rick. "I think we'll try our plan out now."

Rick nodded. "I think you're right. I'll make arrangements to meet with him."

"This one I'll do myself," said Ethan.

"Are you sure? This guy is pretty unstable, and I think you're half the cause," said Rick, concerned.

"Yes, I'm sure. Can you set it up?" asked Ethan.

"Consider it done," said Rick. "When do you want to meet him?"

"Early this afternoon. I want this over now."

"Okay," agreed Rick.

"John, will you be working with us full-time now?" Ethan asked, turning to his new mechanic.

"Part-time for now," John answered. "I feel bad because my boss still needs the help. Plus, it's hard to explain why I'd suddenly quit."

"Don't worry about that," Ethan explained. "I'll make sure he gets some more help, and I'll have someone contact him as your new employer so he doesn't ask questions."

"Thanks," said John. "I appreciate that. I'd much rather work here. Much better pay," he laughed.

"No problem. We're happy to have you on the team," said Ethan.

* * *

As arranged by Rick, Ethan met Alan later that afternoon at a café a few towns away from Belleville. A couple of team members had picked up Alan and taken him there to be sure he didn't miss the meeting.

"I knew there was something funny going on with you," Alan said as he sauntered up to the table. "Tell your goons they need to drive faster. They're wasting my time."

Ethan ignored the comment. "Have a seat," he said, gesturing toward the chair across from him.

"Don't tell me what to do," said Alan, but he sat down obediently. "What do you want?"

"I'll make this brief," said Ethan, pushing an envelope over toward Alan. "You're going to be leaving town and not coming back. You're not going to tell anyone why, and you'll never contact Anna, her friends, or me ever again."

"You can't buy your way out of anything," said Alan, eyeing the envelope greedily. "I love Anna and she will be my wife one day, and no stupid Mr. Wonderful guy is gonna ...." He stopped talking suddenly after opening the envelope, eyeing the paperwork, which detailed a bank account that would be in a business's name, along with Alan's. The balance revealed an exorbitant amount of money. He looked up at Ethan, looking into his eyes to find traces of dishonesty. "Is this real?" he asked. "This is a joke."

"This is no joke, Alan," said Ethan, "and you have five minutes to accept the offer or it's off the table forever."

Ethan had made similar offers before, and greed had always won the recipient over. For most people who threatened to undermine the secrecy of the mansion and its team, greed had been the primary motivator. Knowing that Ethan and his second family lived so comfortably was often a source of jealousy.

But with Alan, Ethan wasn't quite so sure. Although Alan clearly never loved Anna given the way he'd always treated her so poorly-- abusively in fact--Ethan knew that Alan enjoyed a certain amount of control over Anna. Losing that control was what was setting Alan off right now, and Ethan had gambled on a monetary figure that he hoped would overcome that need for power.

It was more money than Alan would hope to make in his lifetime, enough to set himself up very comfortably in some other place that was far, far away. He could buy a house, a car, and live a comfortable lifestyle, but Ethan was still a little uncertain. On the outside, however, he remained as cool and confident as always.

"The clock is ticking," said Ethan. "And you should know that this offer is cancelled if you don't move far away within a week. I never want to see your face again, and if I do, the bank account goes away instantly." The account was designed as a trust in a business name, so Alan couldn't just withdraw all the money and leave. "You'll have a contact who will cosign whenever you need money out of it, no questions asked, as long as you abide by the agreement to stay away."

Alan eyed the paperwork again and excitement built up in his eyes. "Heh, you can have the bitch," he said. "Who wants that whiny brat when I can have all the women I want?" Alan's smile grew the more he thought about his newfound riches. "I'll start packing. Now call your goons and get me out of here."

"They're waiting for you outside," said Ethan calmly, relieved to watch Alan walk out the door. He got up and paid the cashier, including a generous tip, then headed home.

* * *

"He's gone for good," Anna read as she saw her text from Ethan. "I'll explain tonight at dinner."

"That's wonderful!" Anna texted back, wondering what had happened, but relieved because she trusted that Ethan had taken care of the situation.

Soon after, Kelly called Anna. "What's happening at Alan's house?" she asked.

"I don't know, why?" Anna asked.

"There's a huge moving truck parked there!" Kelly exclaimed.

"That's wonderful! Ethan took care of it somehow. I'll find out tonight and let you know."

"Good riddance," said Kelly with a laugh.

With her curiosity piqued, Anna decided to head over to Ethan's a bit early.

CHAPTER TWENTY-NINE

Ethan and Anna were thrilled to be together again, falling into each other's arms as he met her at her car.

"I missed you so much, Ethan!" Anna exclaimed.

"And I missed you, my beautiful Anna, so very much," said Ethan, barely finishing the sentence before their lips met with a long and passionate kiss. Their lips parted but their arms stayed interlocked, squeezing each other tightly, happy that they were back in each other's embrace.

"How was your trip? And what did you do to Alan? Will he bother us anymore? What happened?" Anna greeted him with a barrage of questions, anxious to know everything after their brief time apart.

Ethan chuckled, "Walk with me, and I'll try to answer everything." He took her hand and led her toward the elevator, where they descended into the mansion's main hallway. "The business meeting went well, and we landed the client. I just wish they'd been good with making the deal on a video conference, but the owner of that company is really old-fashioned," he explained as they strolled along the mansion's hallways.

"That's good," Anna said. "I guess not everyone is ready to embrace technology."

"No, especially these people. But it's okay, because the project is going to help a lot of people get into affordable housing."

"That's wonderful," said Anna.

Ethan stopped walking, facing her and taking both of her hands in his. "This thing with Alan, I was able to convince him to go away."

"You offered him money," Anna guessed.

"Yes," Ethan confirmed. "I know it's not ideal that he should benefit from the way he's treated you, but Anna, I saw in his eyes that he's a threat to you and to us."

"You met with him yourself? You saw Alan?" said Anna, surprised that Ethan hadn't sent a team member to handle the chore.

"Yes, I had to be sure that he'd truly agree to my terms. And he did," explained Ethan.

"I guess that's not really surprising," said Anna. "He's always been a pretty greedy person. He'd never spend his money on anything but himself. I honestly don't know how I ever got into an actual relationship with that man. We were young, and I thought he would change. He didn't. He just got worse."

"Anna, you never have to explain your past to me. We all make errors in judgement, and I'm sure he said a lot of things to fool you," Ethan said.

"Yes, he did. And he got worse slowly. It sort of all happened over time, and by then it felt to me like it was too late. It was Kelly who finally helped me get out. She had been warning me about him all along, but somehow I thought that she wasn't seeing the side of him that I did. Of course, she was right."

"I owe Kelly all my happiness for getting you away from that monster," Ethan said.

"Well, now you've sealed the deal. Do you think he'll come back after he's spent it all?" she asked.

"No, I set it up as a trust fund, which I'll replenish if it gets low. He doesn't know that, though. And if he comes back, he's cut off from the fund. He knows that. We've done this sort of thing before and it works out pretty well for everyone," Ethan explained.

"Good. Now let's stop talking about him forever," Anna smiled.

"Agreed," he said. "It's a little early for dinner. What would you like to do?"

"I'd love to check in with the team," she said. "I have a few more ideas for that school Cliff's team was working on."

"Let's go." He gestured for her to take the lead with a smile as they headed down the hallway.

Back in the communications room, Anna spoke with Cliff for a bit, downloading some notes she'd added to her phone over the past few days. Her expertise in teaching had proven to be a great asset to the project, and her new ideas would help them build a curriculum that would embrace the local culture. While Anna talked with the team, Ethan checked in on a few other projects until it was time for dinner, when they both said goodnight to the team and headed down the hallway toward Ethan's private suite.

"We're not going to the dining room?" Anna asked.

"I have a surprise for you," Ethan told her as he opened the door. The sitting area had been rearranged into an intimate dining atmosphere, complete with gently flickering candles, elegant dishes and stemware, and beautiful table linens. Soft music played lightly in the background.

"Ethan, this is wonderful!" exclaimed Anna. "You've outdone yourself."

"Well, I'm afraid this is all Louise," he explained with a laugh. "She's a genius with things like this. I thought we'd have dinner alone tonight. We have plenty of time to eat with the team on other days. But I missed you so much." He explained, reaching for a bottle chilling in a silver ice bucket. "Would you like a drink?" he asked. "This is a great vintage from a family winery in Italy," he added.

"Well, I certainly won't pass that up," she said. Anna didn't often drink alcohol, especially after the years she'd spent with Alan and his uncontrollable drinking, but she did love the taste of a fine wine now and then.

Ethan unscrewed the cork and poured two glasses, handing one to Anna.

"Thank you," she said. "You're so amazing."

"Not half as amazing as you. To us," he said as he raised his glass for a toast.

"To us."

Louise had left a gourmet dinner prepared by Chef Benjamin on warming dishes, so the couple helped themselves to the delicious meal. After finishing a fabulous dessert, Ethan rose and took her hand. "Care to dance?" he asked.

"I'd love to," she answered, taking his hand and rising, moving closer until their bodies touched and swayed gently to the smooth, relaxing music that filled the room. Ethan held her tight for a moment, then gently met her lips with his own, Anna's body melting into the kiss. They made their way to the bed, quickly becoming more passionate until they were almost frantically removing each other's clothes, desperate to become one after their long night apart for Ethan's trip. For hours they made love, at first with a forceful passion and later, as their desires were satisfied, becoming more of a tender embrace until they finally nestled nearly breathlessly in each other's arms. They held each other quietly for several moments, hearing nothing but each other's heartbeats.

"Ethan," she said finally.

"Yes?"

"I have more questions," she said.

He laughed, and Anna joined him. "Well, It's just that I've been wondering," she said.

"About what?"

"Well, it's clear what the mission is here, and how important it is. But I'm still not understanding why we have to be so secretive about it. Why are we still underground and not telling anyone about it all?"

Ethan shifted his body to sit up slightly in the pillows, still embracing Anna gently. "That's a legitimate question. You didn't see how things were before, so I guess it would be hard to understand. It's just the way there was the constant hounding by the media and anyone else who wanted money. I mean, I understand that many people are desperate and need help, but the way it was before, it was hard to see who was truly in need. Plus, there were a lot of … well, unscrupulous women hanging around."

Anna laughed, sitting up a bit. "Well, you can hardly blame them really," she teased.

Ethan laughed as well. "Well I didn't have you, and I didn't think I could ever find you with all those distractions around. It's more than that. It's all just really hard to explain," he said as he stopped to think for a bit. "I guess I have to show you."

"Show me?

"Yes. I said I'd take you to LA. Let's do it soon, and I'll show you why we did things this way."

"When?" she asked.

"Can you go this weekend?"

"I think so. I'm finishing up with helping at school, so I should be free for the summer by the end of the week," Anna said.

"I'll make arrangements," Ethan said.

"I can't wait to go! Can I meet your parents?" she asked.

"Of course. It'll be fun," he said as they snuggled back down tightly in each other's arms. "I love you, Anna," he added.

"I love you, too, Ethan," she said, already excited at the prospect of their trip together.

CHAPTER THIRTY

KELLY PRACTICALLY SQUEALED when she heard of the plans for Ethan and Anna's trip. "You're going to have so much fun!" she told her friend. "I wish I could go, but I know this has to be just for you lovebirds," she added.

"Someday, we'll all go on plenty of trips together," Anna said.

"Oh my! I just realized you'll be flying on a private jet!" Kelly exclaimed.

"Yes, that's definitely something new. And I've never really flown much," Anna said. "Oh, my goodness, what if I throw up right there on a beautiful private jet?!"

Kelly laughed. "You won't throw up. You've never been bothered by flying before, it won't start now on a plane that'll be even more comfortable than a commercial jet."

"I hope you're right."

"Of course I'm right," Kelly said. "So how much did they bribe Alan to get his annoying butt out of town?"

Anna was surprised. "How did you know?"

"How else are they going to drag that greedy little twirp out of Belleville and away from our lives?" Kelly asked with a giggle.

"I don't know how much exactly. But a lot. Ethan wanted to make sure he was gone."

"That's good, but I sure wish he didn't get to live high on the hog after the way he treated you over the years," Kelly said.

"Me, either, and honestly that bothered me at first, too. But really it doesn't matter as long as he's gone."

"Will he come back?" Kelly asked.

"No, apparently Ethan set things all up with a trust fund, so he'll get cut off if he tries anything."

"Brilliant!" Kelly exclaimed.

"Yeah. I honestly think we're done worrying about Alan Shangle."

"Thank god," Kelly added.

* * *

For the rest of the week, Anna had a joyful smile on her face. Everyone around her noticed the spring in her step, including the students at school, and the feeling was contagious. It seemed like everyone in Belleville had a reason to be in a good mood that summer.

Alan's house sat empty for only about a week until it was rented out to a young family, who quickly cleaned up the yard and added some pleasant decorations. As it turned out, both the husband and wife were excellent mechanics, and before long they were both working in Ted Johnston's shop.

"Was this your doing?" Anna asked Ethan one night.

"Guilty as charged," Ethan said with a smile. "And no, they're not going to have to live on those low wages that man pays. I mean, I know he works hard and doesn't make a lot of profit, so I've supplemented their incomes. And I hear they'll be buying the house soon. They're loving Belleville," he added.

"That's wonderful," she said.

* * *

ONE DAY TOWARD THE END OF THE WEEK, LOUISE APPROACHED ANNA.

"My dear, do you have any formal gowns for your trip?" Louise asked her.

"I have one or two," Anna said thoughtfully. "But I hadn't thought of that before. I guess we'll probably be out on the town a lot in LA."

"Yes, probably almost every day. I'm sure Ethan will take you shopping when you're there, but you'll want to have some of your wardrobe ready ahead of time."

"You're right, I'm sure. I think I'll ask Kelly to go shopping. Would you like to come?" Anna asked.

"Oh, I'd love to go another time, thank you. But enjoy this time with your friend for now."

"Are you sure? We'd love to have you along."

"Thank you, dear," said Louise. "But I'm very busy with things around here all week with the trip preparations. Oh, and here, take this," she said, handing Anna a plastic credit card with her name on it.

"Oh, I couldn't accept this. I can't have Ethan buying me everything," Anna said.

"I knew you'd say as much, and this isn't from Ethan. It's a team member card, and you're part of the team. We all need to have a variety of outfits for different occasions like charity galas. Get whatever you need for the trip, and get something for Kelly, too," Louise added.

"Thank you," Anna said with a smile.

* * *

BACK HOME, ANNA DECIDED TO DO A LITTLE RESEARCH ON THE nightlife scene in LA to see what kind of outfits most women were wearing, so she did a few internet searches. Looking over the society news, suddenly she saw Ethan in all his handsome glory, strolling into an office building wearing a very smart and well-tailored suit. The caption read like celebrity gossip: "Where is billionaire Ethan Greenfield going - and where has he been?"

Anna smiled. 'He's been with me,' she thought. She studied the picture closely. The look on Ethan's face was polite, but clearly unhappy, as though he had been caught off-guard. 'I guess I'll learn more about all that soon,' she thought.

She scrolled through a few more pages. The fashions were different at the local clubs compared with some of the charity balls and other high-end events, but overall the dresses were more revealing than Anna had ever felt comfortable in. She texted a couple of links to Kelly.

"I guess that's what I'll be wearing," she told her friend.

"Wow, Anna! You don't see anything like this in Belleville!" Kelly texted back, adding a shocked face emoji followed by a laughing one. "Don't worry. We'll get you fixed up!" a second text said.

* * *

Kelly and Anna drove to Bluewater for their shopping trip, knowing there were few options in the sleepy little town of Belleville for the kind of formal - and sexy - clothes that Anna would need in LA. They spent the whole afternoon trying on several different outfits until they'd found the perfect styles for some fancy LA nightlife. Anna wasn't so sure about one choice.

"Kelly, I've never worn anything so short and so tight in my life," Anna told her friend.

"Oh, stop worrying. This'll knock his socks off," Kelly laughed. "You don't know anyone there. It's a perfect opportunity to try something brave and bold."

"I guess you're right," Anna said reluctantly.

"And you look incredible," Kelly added with a reassuring smile.

By the time they arrived home, the women had several packages to unload into Anna's house, the two women laughing and smiling after a fun and relaxing day.

"I'd better get going so you can get ready," said Kelly. "Thank you so much for the dresses. You know you didn't have to get me anything."

"You looked incredible in them, Kelly," said Anna. "John needs to see you like that. Tell him to take you out to dinner while I'm gone."

"Oh, don't you worry, these outfits won't go to waste," Kelly reassured her.

After Kelly left, taking Sammy with her so she could take care of Anna's cat at her house, it was a busy night of packing for Anna as she got ready. Ethan arrived later and loaded all her bags in the car.

"You've really outdone yourself with shopping," he joked.

"I hope I didn't buy too much."

"I'm just kidding," he said. "We'll be very busy there and you'll need it all."

Back at the mansion, they had a quick dinner with the team before retiring to Ethan's room, their lovemaking a bit quicker that night as they prepared to leave early for their trip.

CHAPTER THIRTY-ONE

ANNA WAS nervous as they drove up to the airport. Leaving the ground always felt so unsafe, and she had only taken a couple of plane trips in her life when she visited relatives. Ethan held her hand, sensing her uncertainty as they approached the private section of the airfield.

As they boarded the plane, Anna was amazed at the wide, comfortable seats and open spaces that reminded her more of an RV than an airplane.

"I guess I didn't know what to expect," she said. "This is incredible."

"I'm always pretty impressed with it myself," said Ethan. "I spent a lot of years taking commercial flights with my family as we built the business."

"Everything is a window seat," she observed.

"Yes, there are great views from anywhere, and you can move around once we're in flight," he explained.

The thought of being in flight made her wince slightly, but Ethan led her to a couple of side-by-side seats so he could comfort her through the takeoff.

The plane started to taxi out to the runway, and Anna felt more relaxed than she had imagined, comfortably close to Ethan's body with his warm fingers interlocked in hers. She even watched out the window as the plane climbed into the clouds and flashed a smile as she turned to Ethan.

"Thank you," she said. "That was kind of fun, actually."

"A plane taking off into the air is an amazing experience," he said.

After several hours they arrived in Los Angeles, and soon they were getting into a limousine while the driver loaded up their bags.

"It's the LA experience," Ethan explained when she gave him a look that suggested the limo was too extravagant.

"I guess I'll get used to it," she laughed.

Los Angeles was unlike anywhere Anna had ever visited. From her view in the limousine, it was hard to see far beyond the immediate streetscapes, but everywhere there was a buzz of activity and excitement that somehow allowed Anna to feel the city's vast scale. She was happy that she wasn't driving, because the sheer volume of traffic would have required full concentration and kept her from enjoying the sights. The areas they passed on the way to their hotel were very similar to what she'd viewed online when looking for fashion choices, and Anna was relieved that she wouldn't be a bit out of place wearing her new clothes.

For Ethan, LA was a familiar and sometimes tedious experience, so his eyes were on Anna. Watching her was the only new experience for him in the city, and the way her eyes sparkled at every new discovery was energizing to him.

When they entered the hotel, they paused only briefly at the front desk, where all arrangements seemed to be taken care of and the staff knew Ethan by name.

"Dean will show you to your room," the smiling concierge explained, "and we'll have your bags up shortly."

"Thanks, Beth," said Ethan. "I stay here every time. I was just here for that last deal," he explained to Anna.

Hardly a moment passed when a group of people rushed forward and started taking pictures and asking Ethan questions.

"Are you staying long in LA?"

"Can you comment on the deal with Delegant, Inc.?"

"Who is this lovely woman with you, Mr. Greenfield?"

Ethan politely waved them off, saying, "I'll answer your questions at the children's hospital gala."

Dean, the hotel staff member who was leading them to their room, guided them forward, largely ignoring the crowd of people and the flash of cameras behind them.

When they entered their room, Anna was impressed. It was a large suite on one of the upper floors, accessed by a private elevator. Everything glistened from floor to ceiling in the huge sitting area that looked large enough to host a small party.

"I'm sorry about that," Ethan said as soon as they were alone. "That's just one of the things that I'm here to show you. I get some pretty unrelenting media attention that makes it hard to even think. There's never time to be alone."

"You don't have to apologize. I sort of knew that would happen, just wasn't quite expecting it so soon," Anna said.

"It'll get worse," he laughed. "But in the meantime, I forgot to warn you. Let's just stick with your first name and be a little vague about where you're from so these people don't overwhelm all the good citizens of Belleville."

She laughed. "Yes, that's probably a good idea. But it is kind of fun getting all that attention."

"It is. At first," he said. "Come on, let's check out the view."

"Oh, I bet it's incredible," she said. Reaching the balcony, she let out a quick breath. "It's stunning," she added.

"Yes, I never get tired of this part," he said. "It's breathtaking, a pure feat of humanity. I love the peace and quiet of the country, but this is amazing, too, with so many people joining together in community."

"Breathtaking is a great word for it," Anna agreed.

The hotel staff knocked on the door, and several people brought in their bags, taking them all the way into the back rooms where Anna assumed the bedroom and bathroom would be.

After tipping the staff, Ethan turned to Anna. "I hate to rush you, but there is a big charity event tonight, the one I was talking about to the reporters. So we'd better start getting ready," he said.

"Oh, I didn't know we'd be busy already."

"Yes, I'm sorry. I should have warned you about that on the plane. We've got a pretty full itinerary for the weekend." They both walked down the hallway toward the bedroom suite. "Here's our bedroom," he said as he smiled and watched her gaze around the room.

"It's beautiful," she said, taking in the luxurious tapestries and bed linens that added elegance to the room. The bedroom was immense and had a small sitting room that connected to a large dressing area, which then led to the bathroom chamber beyond.

She turned to face Ethan and he took her in his arms, both of their bodies relaxing as they melted into a passionate kiss.

"How long do we have?" she asked with a smile.

"Long enough," he said, gazing into her eyes as they once again locked into a passionate embrace.

CHAPTER THIRTY-TWO

THEIR BUSY ITINERARY hadn't left much time for afternoon lovemaking. In no time, Anna and Ethan were dressed to the hilt, Ethan in a black tailored suit and Anna in a strapless blue evening gown, her flowing reddish hair twisted into a stylish updo.

Their limo was downstairs waiting and whisked them off to the charity gala that was held several blocks away. Anna wouldn't have minded a stroll along the downtown area, but Ethan had explained the importance of important donors like him arriving by car.

"Unfortunately, most people think of charity as a way to look good. It's all about themselves. Part of the perks of donating is participating in a fancy arrival experience where everyone takes pictures of you. It's stupid, but if I mess that up for others it affects how much money they give the charity. In the end, I have to keep up appearances for the greater good."

"It sounds like a big responsibility," Anna observed.

"Too big. Frankly, it takes away from the actual good we're doing. I don't need a charity ball at all. I'd rather give money directly or by physically helping with something and just skip all these fancy galas completely. But then, any meaningful fundraising would be impossible for the children's hospital," he explained.

"That's terrible," she said. "I have to admit, though. This is awfully exciting, getting to dress up for a party."

"It's lots of fun at first, until it just starts becoming tedious. That's what I wanted to show you," Ethan said.

Their arrival at the event was just like a red-carpet walk for movie stars, with cameras flashing and questions shouted out from the huge crowd that lingered on the other side of the robe barriers. In fact, Anna noticed quite a few familiar looking people that she thought might be actors on some of the TV shows she watched. She didn't often make much time for television, so she wasn't sure, since she preferred books and outdoor or social activities for entertainment.

But she did love all the attention. When Ethan and Anna walked down the carpet, all eyes were on them. It was electrifying to be the central focus for the crowd, as though Anna was a movie star herself. For a while, she let herself pretend that she was. It wasn't hard to imagine, being on the arm of such a handsome man like Ethan.

When they reached a certain spot, the carpet opened to a wider area with branded banners announcing the gala, the children's hospital charity, and the event's sponsors. Even though Anna was inexperienced in LA customs, it was clear to her they were expected to linger and pose for photos there. As the cameras flashed, many of the same questions that they'd heard in the hotel lobby were fired toward the couple.

Ethan answered most of them with charm and confidence, introducing Anna as "his lovely lady" but sticking to her first name as they had discussed. He ignored other questions about where she was from and instead shifted the focus to the charity.

"We're thrilled to be a part of this effort to add a new cancer ward to the city's children's hospital. We hope to become more involved in the future to help advance research into childhood diseases. We won't be through until every child can enjoy the carefree life they deserve," he stated to the crowd. Everyone cheered and the cameras flashed more as Ethan and Anna entered the gala.

It was held in a magnificent grand ballroom with intricately carved wood trim and exquisite chandeliers flowing gracefully down from the tall ceiling. It was quieter than the crowd outside, but the room was buzzing with conversation.

"Ethan!" cried a blonde, blue-eyed woman who nearly ran to greet him. "It's been ages! We must catch up sometimes."

"Yes, Ellen, that would be nice," said Ethan politely. He then introduced Anna, after which Ellen quickly found a reason to move on, hollering "Devon!" to the next man she saw.

Anna laughed. "That was interesting," she said.

"That's only the beginning," he laughed.

Even after they were seated at their table, Ethan and Anna were constantly approached by a myriad of people hoping to capture Ethan's attention. About half of them were men and women looking to steal a moment of Ethan's time for their latest business idea pitch, but it was the other half who bothered Anna the most. Women of all shapes, sizes, and even ages approached Ethan constantly, despite how closely Anna sat by him and how attentive he was to Anna. They constantly interrupted Ethan and Anna's conversations, seeming to throw themselves at Ethan without caring that he clearly had a relationship with his date.

The madness calmed down considerably when the formal festivities began, which included several speeches, recognition for major donors--including Ethan--and a short awards ceremony for community leaders. But once the crowd was again permitted to mingle, a barrage of people seemed to almost spring up on Ethan out of nowhere. Anna tried to keep up with the small talk, but it just became overwhelming.

* * *

Both Anna and Ethan were happy to finally return to their quiet hotel suite.

"I'm exhausted!" Anna exclaimed. "I don't think I could have lasted another minute there."

"It's like that every night, just about," Ethan explained. "My schedule is full of events like that and I can't even relax at all."

"Can't you just decline the invitations?"

"It's not that easy," he explained. "My family is expected to be a part of the community, and you have to continually participate or you won't be on the committees that make the big decisions. Believe me, I've tried. I've found that if I let everyone else decide on community development, the people who most need the help end up with the short end of the stick."

"Exhausting," she said as she plopped down on the bed, still in her evening gown.

"Are you too exhausted for… everything?" he asked with a smile.

She laughed and reached out her arms. "No, not everything!"

* * *

The next day, Ethan showed her the sights of LA, including the coastal areas, which seemed to have people everywhere enjoying the sunny weather, the downtown area where his company was head-quartered, and even the city's residential areas. "This," he explained, "is the heart of the city. Its people are its soul. You have to see every different part of this city to truly understand it."

That evening, Ethan showed Anna LA's nightlife scene, and she decided to be brave and wear the tight, short dress she'd bought in Bluewater, letting her wavy reddish hair flow naturally.

"You look amazing," he told her as he took her in his arms for a romantic kiss.

"Kelly said you'd like it," she said.

"Every day, I get more and more reasons to like Kelly," he said with a laugh.

The downtown clubs were loud and vibrant, filled with unre-lenting energy. Anna noticed that while many celebrities--and she had noticed quite a few more in her tour of LA--seemed to get less attention than Ethan. While celebrities were wealthy, people were used to seeing them. It was billionaires like Ethan who captured the minds of people who wished to be like him, and they'd flock to him hoping that one day they would be just like him. There were still the occasional business proposals, but out in the clubs, it was the women who flocked to Ethan in droves. They were even more forward in the clubs than they had been at the gala, making overt passes at Ethan while Anna stood right there. Ethan rebuffed or ignored every single one, answering their flirtations by simply giving more of his attention to Anna. Some of the women were downright rude, but Ethan kept his composure and remained polite.

Back in their hotel room that night, Anna and Ethan headed to bed again, exhausted.

"This has been crazy," Anna said.

"Yes, and it's only been two nights," Ethan observed. "It never stops. It really doesn't."

"I'm beginning to see that now," she said, sliding into his arms. "But anywhere I am and anything I'm doing, it's so much better because you're with me."

"I love you, Anna," he whispered.

"I love you, too, Ethan," she said breathlessly as their lips met in a kiss.

CHAPTER THIRTY-THREE

ANNA FELT WELL-RESTED the next morning. She was still excited about being in LA with Ethan, but the lifestyle in his circles was too intense for her small-town tastes.

Today, Ethan planned to take Anna to see more of the sights, so they both dressed casually. There was another formal event held that evening, this time a benefit for literacy. Ethan's company was a major sponsor, so Ethan's parents would also attend.

This would be the first time Anna would be meeting Ethan's parents, and it was going to happen at a formal event. Anna was grateful that she could dress up for the occasion, since otherwise she wouldn't have a clue what to wear if invited to the Greenfields' private home. However, she also felt that meeting the parents was a big step in any relationship, so she was a bit nervous about it happening at a formal event in front of a bunch of strangers.

For now, she turned her thoughts to the afternoon itinerary, which had Ethan and Anna visiting some of the local LA attractions. The big theme parks would wait for another trip. Because Anna had always wanted to visit them, she had asked Ethan not to plan them for the weekend trip since they would be too rushed to enjoy them. Instead, Ethan planned for the couple to visit local art museums and other destinations that would give Anna a taste of the community culture.

The first stop was a destination all in itself: a library, a museum, and a botanical garden all in one. Ethan held Anna's hand as they strolled around the gardens. Because it covered many acres, they were only able to see a couple of the main exhibits, including a gorgeous display by Chinese artisans and a Shakespearean garden with an English countryside theme.

It wasn't long before Ethan was recognized. A group of women marched up and started trying to get Ethan's attention. A tall blonde complemented Anna on her looks, all the while focusing her eyes on Ethan, who remained polite but eventually convinced the group to leave. With all the commotion, neither Ethan nor Anna noticed the man with short blonde hair and blue eyes standing nearby. He was looking at the flowers, but frequently shifted his eyes to gaze at Ethan and Anna.

"I'm so sorry," Ethan said to Anna after the women had left.

"It's not your fault. I'm starting to really see what you mean by wanting to get away from this," she said.

They continued to explore the museum and gardens. With her love of books and learning, Anna was completely enchanted with the library. Its incredible collection of rare books included a Gutenberg Bible, something Anna had never seen in person before.

"I used to come here a lot when I lived here," Ethan told her. "My mother is a patron of the arts and loves to volunteer her time here."

"She sounds lovely," Anna said. "I can't wait to meet her."

"You will soon," he said.

For lunch, the couple ventured out toward the coastline, finding a small locally owned seafood restaurant with a view of the ocean. The food was fresh and delicious, and afterward Anna and Ethan walked along the shoreline of the Pacific Ocean.

The beach was crowded, with people roller skating along the boardwalk and hanging out in small groups. The atmosphere was fun and friendly, with lots of street musicians and artists doing their best to compete for attention. Ethan contributed to the cash funds of every performer he passed, each nodding gratefully as he added his donation to the piles of cash in their buckets or instrument cases.

Anna was sure that there were enough people on the beach to blend in, but Ethan was still recognized everywhere he went, with some people trying to make appointments with him and others just hoping for some more personal attention. Anna was exhausted, and she could tell by the polite, yet impatient, smile on Ethan's face that he had also had just about enough of his popularity.

They were both relieved to be back in the hotel room.

"You know, if they wanted some advice on life or even career advice, I'd be happy to give it," Ethan explained to Anna. "But it always comes back to money. I'm not averse to giving my money away, either, if it's for a good cause. But there's really no way to know. And they won't leave me alone until the answer is yes, regardless of whether it will benefit others."

"It's exhausting," Anna agreed, looking at the time. "I'd better get ready for tonight. Care to join me in the shower?" she asked with a smile.

"I'd be honored," laughed Ethan as they headed past the dressing area.

The rainwater shower was a luxury Anna had not experienced before. It reminded her a lot of the waterfall that greeted her whenever she went down the elevator to the underground mansion. But this one was better. It was warm and refreshing, and she and Ethan could be together in it.

Ethan turned to her and put his lips to hers, gently at first, then with building passion. He lowered her straps down her shoulders gently, moving his arms to the back to unzip her sundress. At the same time, she pulled up his shirt and they both helped take it off, then she reached down to undo his belt. Soon they were both under the gentle rain of the shower, Ethan leaning Anna against the smooth marble walls as he kissed her and ran his hands all over her body. He lifted her up and onto him as they made love, the water gently beading on their skin.

"We do need to get ready," she laughed when they had finished making love.

"I thought that's what we were doing," he said as he reached for the bottle of shampoo and gently massaged her flowing wet hair.

"That feels good," she said, returning the favor, although it was a bit challenging since he was so much taller.

When they got out of the shower, the couple got ready for the evening's charity event. Anna dressed in the green gown she had worn for their date at the theater, and Ethan chose a dark grey suit that complemented Anna's look perfectly. For this event, she left her hair flowing with delicate blow-dried waves and wore simple diamond jewelry to finish the look.

"You look stunning," he said. "We still have a few minutes. Would you like a drink? We can head down to the bar."

"I'd love a glass of wine," she said, and he took her hand and led her to the elevator.

CHAPTER THIRTY-FOUR

Anna and Ethan exited the elevator in the lobby and walked hand-in-hand to the hotel's bar. It was a high-end establishment with elegant marble surfaces and bright gold accents that sparkled in the dim, romantic lighting.

The couple sat at a table near the bar area. It wasn't crowded, being just before the dinner hour rush, but a few patrons were starting to fill up the bar area. The atmosphere was formal yet friendly, and Anna thought it was a pleasant place to be, but Ethan looked around a bit cautiously.

"Anything wrong?" she asked him.

"No, everything is fine," he said, turning to her. "I'm just waiting for the swarm," he laughed.

"I expect that won't take long," Anna said with a smile.

Sure enough, the couple had barely ordered drinks when a tall, dark haired man approached Ethan.

"Mr. Greenfield? That's you, right?" he said.

"Yes," Ethan answered patiently. "I'm Ethan Greenfield. What can I do for you?"

"I hate to bother you," the man began, and Ethan cringed in his mind, although outwardly he maintained a cordial composure. These conversations always opened with how much the approaching person hated to bother him, yet they always managed to do just that. Ethan was a patient man, but after years of the constant barrage of business offers and ideas, not to mention all the doting women looking for his attention, maintaining that patience was something he had to continually work at.

The man continued, "I have a wonderful idea for a tech start-up. I was wondering if I could set up a time to meet with you this week?"

"Unfortunately, I'm only in Los Angeles for another day," explained Ethan. He reached into his wallet and handed the man a business card. "This is my assistant's number. He will be happy to video conference with you about it. Just call him and set up an appointment."

"Oh, thank you, that will be great," said the man. "I'll leave you to your drinks, then. So sorry to bother you. Thank you again."

"You're very welcome," said Ethan. The man walked away with a smile on his face, and he even seemed to have an extra spring in his step.

"You've made his day," laughed Anna.

"I hope I did. I gave him Cliff's card. Hopefully it's a good idea, and Cliff doesn't want to whack me when I get home," he said. They both laughed. "I really want to help people, so I try to be there for them and listen to them. Lots of people have great ideas, they just never get a chance to implement them. I want to give people a chance, but I just simply don't have time for everybody," he said with a faraway look.

"Ethan, you're a wonderful man. You do what you can for people, much more than most other men in your position. You can't be there for everyone, so you can't beat yourself up over that," Anna said, laying her hand on Ethan's.

"You're right. And intellectually, I know that. But it still really affects me when I don't have time for people. I feel like I'm missing the one person with the great idea that will help make the world better."

"That's possible, but there's still nothing more you can do. You give of yourself every day," she said.

"It's the reason I moved away. So many people constantly trying to get my attention. It takes a toll on emotions, not being able to be there for everyone," he explained.

"I can understand that," she said.

"I tried moving away before, like you had talked about. Just moved away and went on with my life. It didn't take long for the media to find me, then suddenly there was everyone again, coming at me from every which way until I was… well, frankly I was overwhelmed." He looked into Anna's emerald eyes. "I've never talked to anyone but my parents about these emotions before," he said.

"I love you," she said. "I'll always be here for you for all of this. And I'm starting to understand even more about …" she looked around first before whispering, "about the mansion."

"That's how it came about. Instead of everyone coming up to me and asking for something, we--the team--we go out to the people and find the people with ideas. They're everywhere, all around us. People leading ordinary lives who have extraordinary ideas. But they don't get heard because of all the noise, all the distracting bells and whistles of society that can suck the confidence right out of a person. I just needed a quiet place to think so those ideas could come to life, where I could go to people instead of people always coming to me," he explained.

"You're a wonderful man, Ethan Greenfield," Anna said, and they leaned into each other for a kiss.

"You," he said when they came up for air, "are the woman of my dreams."

"It's you! I thought that was you!" a voice suddenly hollered from behind them. A woman appeared, with deep black, flowing hair wearing a blue silk dress. "Ethan Greenfield. I've seen you in all the society magazines!"

Anna took a sip of her wine to hold back a giggle.

"Hello," said Ethan politely as he gave a sideways glance to Anna and narrowed his eyes. It only made Anna laugh more, so she acted like she was checking her dress so she could turn away.

"It's amazing who you meet when you're in LA. I'm gonna tell all my friends I was rubbing shoulders with none other than Ethan Greenfield!" the woman exclaimed, walking away just as quickly as she came.

"I assure you, my dearest Anna," said Ethan rather formally, "I never rubbed that woman's shoulders."

Unable to hold it in any longer, Anna burst out laughing.

"You see what I go through," Ethan said, joining her laughter.

Anna slowly gained her composure so she could speak again. "You're wonderful," she said.

"As are you, my beautiful Anna," he said. "Now, I think we should head out so we're not late to the charity event."

"Let's go!" exclaimed Anna as she rose from her seat, still giggling as they walked out of the bar.

As they exited the hotel, a man with short sandy hair and blue eyes watched them from the lobby as they entered their limousine.

CHAPTER THIRTY-FIVE

ONCE AGAIN, Anna felt like a movie star when she stepped out of the limousine and walked down the red carpet alongside Ethan. He had an outstanding presence everywhere, but at this event, which was sponsored by his family's company, his strides were just a tad longer and he stood just a little bit taller. Ethan Greenfield, the handsome, eligible bachelor, billionaire CEO, and member of a prominent LA family--Anna felt like a princess on his arm.

And she looked the part. Her emerald-green gown matched the gemstone color of her eyes, the form-fitting dress embroidered with intricate designs in incredibly detailed hand stitching. Her cream-colored skin told the world that the reddish tint of her hair was her natural color, and her understated diamond jewelry added just the right sparkle for a decidedly classic style.

Her smile was wide as Anna entered the exquisite ballroom, which was even more stunning than that of the venue from the night before. She was a little nervous from the knowledge that she would meet Ethan's parents at the event, but outwardly she carried herself as the perfect mix of confidence, beauty, and intellect.

From across the room they spotted them instantly, the larger-than-life couple with practically unlimited California connections,

James and Linda Greenfield. Right away Anna could see traces of both parents in Ethan, having his father's chiseled features and sandy blonde hair as well as his mother's eyes, the perfect mirror image of a bright, blue sky. The parents smiled when they spotted their son from across the room, and Ethan led Anna over to them, his fingers interlaced between hers.

"Ethan!" His mother was the first to speak, taking a few steps forward to welcome her son with a hug. Ethan gracefully dropped Anna's hand to put his arms around his mother. "Hello, Mom," he said, then turned to face Anna. "I'd like you to meet Anna."

"Anna, it's so lovely to meet you," Linda said to her, offering her arm for a half-hug.

"Good to meet you," said Anna, reciprocating the hug, then stepping back to turn to James Greenfield, who had just shaken his son's hand.

"It's wonderful to meet you," James said, taking her hand in both of his as a warm, welcoming gesture.

"Nice to meet you, too," Anna told him, giving a light squeeze to Ethan's father's hands.

"Let's go have a seat so we can talk a little before the festivities begin," suggested James, guiding Anna and the others toward a nearby table for four, where the two couples sat down.

"How long are you in town?" asked Linda.

"Until tomorrow," said Ethan.

"Well, that's much too short for a visit," his mother said with a frown.

"I know. I'm sorry, Mom. We'll plan for a longer stay another time."

"I'm going to hold you to that," said Linda, raising her eyebrows at her son.

"Can I get you two some drinks?" asked James.

"I'll take a bourbon," said Ethan, who then looked over at Anna.

"I think I'd just like an iced tea," she said.

"Me, too, dear," Linda said.

James waved down a waiter and gave the man the order for all four of them, then turned back to his son. "So, tell me what you two have been up to in our fine city."

"I showed her the gallery and the beach. We attended the gala last night, and we haven't had much time for anything more," Ethan answered.

"Oh, I adore the gallery," said his mother.

"I loved it, too. The gardens were lovely, and the library is incredible," said Anna.

"Yes, it is quite extraordinary," said Linda.

"Anna, we've heard so much about you that it feels like we know you already. You're a teacher?" James asked.

"Yes, sixth grade. It's wonderfully rewarding. I love my students," Anna answered.

Their drinks arrived just then, and Ethan sampled the bourbon. "This is good stuff," he said.

"Only the best for this charity. It's one of your mother's favorites," James explained.

Linda smiled and looked lovingly at her husband, then back to Anna. "Dear, I want to hear everything about you."

"I don't know where to start… " began Anna, but just then a sound of clanking glasses came from the event stage. The MC welcomed everyone to the event and said it was time for the festivities to begin.

Linda leaned in to whisper to Anna. "We'll talk later," she said, and Anna nodded and smiled.

The event was a benefit for local literacy groups, and the program included a few speeches, an awards ceremony, and a silent auction, followed by dinner. Being a teacher, Anna found the speakers especially inspiring, and thought she could take many of the ideas expressed back to her classroom to benefit her own students.

Time passed quickly, and soon they were served dinner, when the couples were able to resume their earlier conversations.

Linda and Anna sat together and talked about teaching, since Linda had also been a teacher for a while before she met her husband. Ethan and his father talked mostly business, with Ethan explaining some of his new ideas for the company and James talking about some of the new developments at the LA office.

"You boys only talk about business," Linda chastised her son and husband. "You barely get together. Talk about something fun!"

"Business is fun, dear, when you love what you do," said James with a laugh.

She flashed him a crooked smile and shook her head, then turned back to Anna. "Men," she told her, "They don't know how to relax and have fun."

Anna laughed.

The night wore on and the event ended, with people filing out the door as Ethan, Anna, and his parents talked more.

A man walked up to the table. "We did great tonight, James," he told Ethan's father. "Had lots of great donations for the charity."

"That's wonderful," said James, who turned to Anna. "This is my assistant, Thomas."

"Hello Thomas," she said.

"A pleasure to meet you, Miss," said Thomas.

As the hotel staff began to clean up, Ethan's parents walked Anna and Ethan out to their limousine.

"I'm going to miss you, son," said Linda, giving Ethan a tight hug.

"I'll miss you, too, Mom. But you know we video chat every day," he laughed.

"It's not the same," she insisted with a pout.

James gave his son a handshake and put his hand on his shoulder. "We'll talk soon," he told him, then turned to Anna. "Anna, it was an absolute pleasure to meet you tonight," he said, taking her hand as he did when he first greeted her.

"The pleasure has been all mine," she said.

His parents waved goodbye as they drove away, and Anna kept looking back until she saw James tenderly take his wife's hand and lead her over toward their own car.

"Your parents are so lovely," she said.

"Yes, they're wonderful. They've really been understanding about my decision to move away, and they've been so supportive. They actually have fun throwing misleading hints to the media about where I might be when I'm not in LA," he told her.

"I can see Linda doing that!" she laughed.

They headed back to the hotel for a quiet night alone in their suite before leaving for the airport the next day and flying back to the underground mansion in Belleville.

CHAPTER THIRTY-SIX

THE FEELING WAS bittersweet as Anna and Ethan arrived at the airport. She had wished they'd had more time to spend with his parents. Anna had been surprised at how comfortable she'd felt around the Greenfields - it was as if she had known them for a lifetime. Anna had also wished she could have gone to some of the city's other attractions, although she certainly didn't miss all the people who constantly came around vying for Ethan's attention.

This time, she wasn't nervous about the takeoff at all, having just experienced the flight on the private jet only a couple of days ago. She nestled into Ethan's arms and felt so comfortable against his strong, warm body that she even fell asleep for a while.

The plane landed smoothly, and Anna and Ethan headed to the parking garage to retrieve Ethan's car. They drove home holding hands as Anna watched the peaceful fields of green pass by, the breeze sending ripples across the crops, fanning out like waves across a country lake.

"What a difference," she observed.

"Yes, the peacefulness here is something to behold. I love the city, but this … this feels almost spiritual."

"I know what you mean," she said, locking her fingers into his.

They arrived at Ethan's property and entered the underground parking garage.

"Do you have some time, or would you like to get back?" he asked.

"I have plenty of time. Kelly has Sammy, so I don't have to worry about feeding him or anything," she said. "Speaking of that...." She brought out her phone for a quick text to Kelly to tell her she was back in town, but that she wouldn't be home yet.

"Have fun!" texted Kelly, adding a smiley face emoji.

Ethan and Anna's first stop was to see the pets, and Teddy the German Shepherd ran forward to greet Ethan. Tara had just been playing fetch with him, and he dropped his ball to lick Ethan all over.

Anna laughed and gave the dog a big, tight hug. "We missed you!" she told him.

They spent a little while in the pets' room relaxing on the sofas and throwing the ball for Teddy. Milo climbed down from his perch on the massive wall structure to come sit on Anna's lap for a few pets before he went back to his climbing. The dog eventually laid down for a rest, and Anna and Ethan decided to go to the lounge to relax some more before dinner.

"I'd like you to meet my parents, too," Anna said as she swirled around the ice in her glass of tea.

"I'd love to. Should we have them over here for dinner?" he asked.

"I think so, but they'll need to be prepared a bit, and we'll have to bring them over early so they're not still in shock when dinner time comes," she laughed.

"Good idea," he agreed, smiling. "You up for a game of pool?" he asked, nodding toward the pool table.

"Sure. But I need to warn you, I'm pretty good," she said with a grin.

"Oh, well, then," he said, "Challenge accepted."

"We didn't bet anything, silly," she said.

"How about this," he said. "The loser has to tell Cliff that I gave his number to that guy."

She laughed. "That's not a good bet. You know that guy probably already bugged him."

"Okay. How about winner gets to choose dessert?"

"That's my kind of bet," she said. "Prepare to eat apple pie."

They laughed and headed over to the pool table, where Anna went first, landing two solid balls in the pockets on the break.

"I'm in trouble." Ethan laughed.

They played two rounds, with Anna winning the first game and Ethan winning the second.

"Tie breaker?" he asked.

"Let's just leave it where it is," she said. "We'll both choose dessert. But I could use a few pointers on my form," she added with a sly, sexy glance at Ethan.

"Oh, yeah? Well, what you've got to do is lean into it like this...." He wrapped his arms around her from behind, pretending to show her how to hold the cue stick. Anna leaned back into him as he ran his hands gently along her arms, then down her body past her hips. She turned around, dropping the cue, and his hands never left her body as her arms wrapped around him and they met with a passionate kiss. He lifted her up onto the pool table and laid her down as they continued to kiss and caress each other.

"Won't people walk in?" she asked between kisses.

"Probably. Let's get somewhere more private," he said.

They got up and practically sprinted down the hallways until they reached his suite, where he picked her up and carried her through the doorway and laid her on his bed. Their clothes came off quickly, each helping the other undress with a fury of emotion, each yearning to be a part of the other. They joined in romantic embrace, gently at first, then with escalating fury until they reached their height of mutual pleasure. Satisfied and exhausted, they both collapsed into the pillows, still gripping tightly onto one another.

"Anna," he said breathlessly.

"Ethan," she said.

"I love you so much."

"I love you more," she said, and they both laughed.

They laid together for a few moments, relaxed and happy, their warm bodies so close and comfortable together.

"I'm hungry," she said finally, and they laughed again.

"I've worked up an appetite myself. I guess we'd better go see what's happening in the dining room," he said.

They rose and got dressed, or tried to, since Anna couldn't find her bra that was lost in the sea of fabric in Ethan's huge bed. He found it first, dangling it in front of her.

"I'd rather just spend the evening lusting over your beautiful naked body," he said with a chuckle, then tossed the bra over to her. She laughed and moved closer to him, bending her head back to give him a peck on his chin, then they both finished getting dressed.

"Let's go get some food," she said.

He smiled and their lips met one more time before they headed out the door for the dining room.

CHAPTER THIRTY-SEVEN

CHEF BENJAMIN and his team had prepared a special dinner to welcome Anna and Ethan home, and several team members joined in the feast.

"Ethan," said Cliff, who was stirring the dressing into his salad.

"Yes?" answered Ethan, pushing around pieces of his own salad with his fork, purposefully not looking at Cliff.

"I got a call yesterday," Cliff said matter-of-factly.

"I imagine you get several calls per day," Ethan said, still not looking up from his plate.

Anna was giggling.

"This particular call was a person who asked for me by name," Cliff said.

"Well, you're a pretty popular guy. Good looks and all…." Ethan said while chasing a golden grape tomato around his bowl.

Cliff laughed. "I'm not mad, actually. Dave's a nice guy and he seems to have some good ideas for his start up. We can probably help him out."

Finally, Ethan looked up. "I knew it all along," he said with a confident smile.

"Next time, though, I'm going to check your wallet before you leave town to make sure you only have your own business cards."

"Deal," said Ethan.

The dinner continued as each of the team members gave an update on what happened to their projects while Ethan and Anna were gone.

"By the way, Anna," said Cliff, "I put a few things on your desk while you were gone. Notes on the school project that I need your input on."

Anna stopped eating and looked up suddenly. "I have a desk?"

"Well… yes…." Cliff said, looking over at Ethan.

"Of course you do, sweetheart. You're a team member now. We wouldn't have come as far as we have on that school project if not for your input. And that's just the start," Ethan explained.

"Well, that's wonderful," Anna said with a smile. "I hope that I really do help you out."

"Of course you do," said Cliff. "That's why there are notes on your desk," he added with a smile.

"Well, thank you. That's wonderful that you include me," she said.

After they finished eating, everyone went their separate ways in the mansion. A few of the staff members were leaving after their shifts, and replacements were expected to arrive soon.

"Where do they go?" Anna asked as she and Ethan strolled down the hallway, watching the people head toward their cars in the garage.

"They all have homes in different places. Some have families that are settled in their own cities, so only the team member stays here. Others bring their families to stay here on their shifts, but that doesn't work for many of them since their spouses also have careers," Ethan explained. "How about you? Are you staying tonight?" he asked, flashing her a sexy smile.

"I want to, but I should get home to get Sammy back. It's kind of a pain for Kelly when they have him, since they have to keep him separate from their little dog. They don't always get along," she said.

"I understand. I don't want to rush you or pressure you into anything, but I want you to know that you're welcome to live here. You and Sammy," he said.

"I know. I've been thinking about that, but I worked so hard for my little house. I'm not quite ready to give it up yet," she said.

"I'd never ask you to give it up. That home will be yours forever," Ethan said.

"I appreciate that. The first really 'adult' thing I ever did was buy that house," Anna explained. "It was a big accomplishment. It's nothing like this place," she waved around her hands to indicate the underground mansion, "but it was a lot to me. It still means a lot to me."

Ethan held both her hands. "I understand completely. I still have my first house, too."

"I want to see it sometime! Thank you. And I'm understanding all this much more, too, after our trip. I can't imagine having to deal with that every single day. For a weekend it's fun, but a little exhausting. For a lifetime, I can't even imagine what you went through," she said.

"It's overwhelming," he said. "And when I finally decided that I wanted to come here, I thought about what it might do to the town. Eventually, they always find me - the media, the paparazzi, the business proposals, the marriage proposals...." They both laughed at the last example. "Can you imagine how they'd trample over our little town?" he added.

"Yes, I can imagine. But it works here, really well. You've created quite a little family here," she said.

"Yes, we're a great group. It's amazing because we always get along so well. Most coworkers eventually get sick of each other. Then there's office politics, and hurt feelings over promotions, all that stuff. None of it happens here. It's amazing," he said.

"It's because no one really works here. They're all just doing what they love," Anna said.

"Exactly. It's a passion. A purpose. And we all work as a team," he said.

"Thank you for making me part of that team," she said, gazing into his sky-blue eyes.

"I wouldn't have it any other way," he said.

They moved closer, the warmth of their bodies blending as their lips met. He led her over to a nearby sofa, where they sat together. He showered kisses across her neck and nuzzled into her, holding her tightly and kissing her passionately.

After several minutes they both rose, and he led her out up the elevator and outside. Daylight was waning, but the hot midsummer sun still lingered long after the dinner hour. Streaks of gold, orange, and red were beginning to take over the sky, tinting the clouds with a light shade of pink. The sky, the fields - they were all expansive, and far in the distance, spread-out farmhouses speckled the landscape. They were the only buildings, other than the tiny vintage farmhouse, that could be seen for miles.

They kissed again at the car, and Ethan embraced her tightly.

"I'll see you tomorrow," he said.

"Tomorrow," she repeated. "I love you, Ethan."

"I love you, Anna."

He lingered for a while outside after she pulled away, watching the sun set into the rolling hills with a wide smile of contentment on his face.

CHAPTER THIRTY-EIGHT

ANNA HAD TEXTED Kelly before leaving Ethan's mansion to tell her she was on her way. She pulled into her friend's driveway and headed to the door. Kelly met her in the doorway, opening it so she could go inside.

"Hi there, stranger!" Kelly exclaimed. "You must sit, and you must tell all before I release your fur baby into your custody."

Anna laughed. "Well, there is a lot to tell. Has he been good?"

"Mister Sammy only shredded one roll of toilet paper, so that's a record," Kelly reported with a laugh.

"Oh, I'm so sorry!" Anna said, chastising her cat as he jumped up in her lap.

"It's nothing. But I must know gossip immediately. Did you wear the dress?" Kelly asked.

"Yes!" Anna squealed. "I can't believe I wore that thing in public. It's practically a piece of lingerie."

John had walked into the room, but he spun around on his heels and headed back out. "Men must exit. Men must exit," he mumbled. Anna laughed.

"You're a big goof," Kelly said to him, then she turned back to Anna. "I bet he loved it," she said.

"Yes, he did."

"Oh, I see," said Kelly. "I'm not going to get details," she laughed.

"Well, let's just say the details are exactly as you'd imagine," Anna said.

"That's wonderful. I'm so happy for you both."

"Oh, and I met his parents," Anna said.

"Wow! What are they like?" Kelly asked.

"Larger than life but down to earth at the same time. I'm not sure that made any sense."

"No, but that's okay," laughed Kelly. "I bet they are wonderful, having raised a son like Ethan."

"Yes, they are. Linda was a teacher, too," Anna said.

"How cool! That means you had a lot to talk about."

"We did, but not a lot of time to do so. We only met on the last night, and it was at a charity event," Anna explained.

"What were those like?" Kelly asked.

Anna went on to explain about the gala and the second charity event, as well as the nightclubs and all the sightseeing she and Ethan had done on their trip.

"I need to go to LA," Kelly laughed.

John ducked his head into the room. "Not without me," he said.

"You're listening, you silly," Kelly said. "I wouldn't want to go without you anyway. It wouldn't be any fun at all without all of us there."

"It's a date!" John exclaimed, then popped out of the room just as quickly.

Anna laughed again. "I'd better get going. I want to get home before it's completely dark and see how my flowers are doing."

"We checked on them. Everything's fine, but I understand," said Kelly. "Here, let me go get his carrier."

Kelly walked away and returned soon with the cat carrier. Anna put Sammy inside and carried him out to the car.

"I finally called Bree while you were gone," Kelly said. "I told her all about you and your gorgeous hunk Ethan."

Anna giggled, her cheeks flushing.

"I didn't tell her about the mansion, don't worry," she added. "She seems convinced that she'll never find the right guy. I told her to hang on. There's always hope."

"There is," Anna agreed. "I'll need to call her again soon and say the same thing."

"Maybe you'll need to invite her to a wedding soon." Kelly raised an eyebrow.

"You're just as silly as John," Anna said. "I'd better get Sammy home. Call you later!"

The friends gave each other a quick hug, then Anna headed home.

Pulling into her driveway, memories of every moment of their trip flooded her mind, especially the intimate moments with Ethan in the hotel bedroom. She looked up at her house before she stepped onto the porch. "You'll be mine forever," she told her little home. "I think Ethan will, too."

She went inside and let Sammy out of his carrier, and he immediately jumped up on his favorite chair.

"I guess that chair comes with us," she said aloud. 'If we move,' she thought. 'And I don't see why I wouldn't move in with Ethan. I really don't want to leave him every night, and it doesn't make sense to just always come home, especially now that I'm part of the team.'

She considered whether she would continue teaching. She loved her students, but she felt like she could reach so many more children with the projects Cliff and the team were working on.

Suddenly a light moved across her curtains, catching her eye and interrupting thoughts of her career. She could hear a car outside and she peeked out the corner of the curtain, being careful not to pull it back too far. A car was indeed driving by, slowly, and it sped up just a little after it passed her house. By then, it was too dark to tell what kind of car it was or what color it was, since she hadn't seen it until it was past the streetlight.

Anna shuddered. 'No, relax Anna,' she thought to herself. 'It can't be Alan. There's no way he would jeopardize all that money. Not that greedy man.' Just in case, she double-checked all her door locks and grabbed her phone.

"A car just drove by. It's probably nothing, but it gave me the creeps," she texted to Ethan.

"I'll be right there," he answered.

"You don't have to do that," she texted back. He didn't answer. "He's already on his way," she said aloud with a smile.

In just a few minutes, Ethan Greenfield was at Anna's front door, and she let him in.

"You didn't have to drive over here," she said. "It was gone in an instant. I doubt it's Alan."

"Me, too. But I just want to be sure," he said. They kissed, then he held her tight.

"A sleepover at your place sounds fun anyway," he said with a laugh. "And I forgot my pajamas, so…." he added with a grin.

"Well, Mr. Greenfield," Anna said very formally. "We'll just have to make do."

She led him to her bedroom.

After they made love, she rested her head on his chest, feeling the rise and fall of his breathing and hearing the gentle beat of his heart. She understood then that their relationship was strong enough that 'place' didn't really matter. It was fluid. Wherever the day took them, their feelings would still be there. They could be in an elaborate underground mansion, a small town house on a quiet city street, a luxury hotel in a big city - it was all the same because their love was the foundation, not the building they were in.

She realized then that Ethan had known that all along, which is why he never pressured her for anything. They were both strong and independent people, and they could lead their lives, have their own careers, be their own people, but their love would be a constant. Like a sturdy rope, their love was the third strand that intertwined with Ethan and Anna to bond the two of them together and make both of them stronger.

She smiled at the thought as she drifted off to sleep, safe in his arms, wondering what tomorrow would bring for them.

CHAPTER THIRTY-NINE

ANNA AND ETHAN woke up together the next morning to find Sammy curled up on their feet.

Ethan laughed. "Well, hello there," he said.

"He always sleeps here," Anna explained, moving to pick him up.

"No, no. He's fine," Ethan said, running his hands over her exposed arm. "Good morning," he said, gazing into her eyes and cupping her cheek with his hand.

"Good morning," Anna said with a smile, and their lips met. She rolled over on top of him to deepen the kiss.

He moaned softly. "If you keep this up, we're getting nothing else done today," he laughed.

"I could live with that," she laughed. "Although we'd probably be letting the team down."

"Yes, we had a whole weekend of fun, so we probably should be joining them to help with the work," he said.

"Alright. Do you want to shower? Or head home first? I guess you should leave some clothes here for sleepovers," she said.

"Hmm," he said thoughtfully, eyeing her with a sexy smile. "You haven't shown me your shower yet."

"I thought you said we needed to get going," she laughed, taking his hand and leading him to the bathroom.

In the shower, they lingered for a few moments to caress each other under the warm water.

"I love showers with you," she said.

He kissed her in response, running his hands down her back and pulling her in close. Then he lifted her up by her thighs and she wrapped her legs around him. They turned, using the shower wall as a brace as they made love.

"I guess we're late," Anna said as soon as they finished, and they both started laughing, finishing up the shower and getting dressed.

On the ride back to the mansion, Anna turned to Ethan. "I've met your parents, and I'd like you to meet mine. Do you think they could come for dinner this week to meet you and see... everything?" she asked.

"Of course," he said. "I'd love that! Tell me which day they can come, and I'll have Chef Benjamin make something extraordinary."

"That will be lovely," she said. "Thank you." She leaned over and kissed him on the cheek as he drove.

* * *

Back at the mansion, they stopped by Ethan's room so he could change, then walked toward the communications room. Ethan stopped just short of the door and led Anna into another room nearby.

It was an office, with an elegant mahogany desk and a leather chair. A few files and some notebooks were stacked neatly on the desk.

"It's a little sparse right now," explained Ethan. "But I figured you'd want to add your own personal touches."

"It's mine?" Anna said, walking inside.

"All yours. I met with the team the other day and we decided that the best title for you is Vice President of Project Management. That is, unless you prefer a c-suite title," said Ethan.

"Vice President? Are you sure that's okay? I mean, all of these people have been here much longer than me. I don't want to take away from anyone's job," she said.

"Of course it's okay," he insisted. "Everyone here has a title that suits their talent, and we all thought you should have something special for yours."

"I guess somewhere along the line I got hired," she laughed.

He laughed, but then put a half frown on his face. "I'm sorry. I guess I never even asked you. I didn't mean to be presumptive. I would never, ever ask you to stop teaching, or in any way try to tell you what to do."

"I know that," she said, giving him a peck on the lips. "I love it. I think it's perfect. And I haven't even made up my mind yet about teaching. I love the kids, but I think I could do more good here. I need some time on that."

"You can do both, if you'd like," he said, then a team member popped his head in the room.

"Ethan," said the man, then he noticed that Anna was there. "Oh, I'm sorry to interrupt."

"No, Sean. We were just finishing up," said Ethan.

"Hi, Anna," said Sean, then he turned back to Ethan. "Our Penglegrove client is insisting that he talk to you right away."

"Go ahead, Ethan," said Anna. "I'll take a look at the notes Cliff gave me," she said, nodding to the papers on her desk.

"I'll see you later," said Ethan, giving her a quick kiss and heading out the room with Sean.

Anna walked over to her desk and ran her fingers on the beautiful wood. It was a quality desk, probably handmade, with intricate carvings and fine details. It was a dark wood, but the desk was far from masculine, with delicate feminine lines. It was perfect, and Ethan had chosen it just for her.

She sat down in the chair, which fit her perfectly, and took out her cellphone to call her parents.

"Mom," she said when her mother answered. "Can you and Dad come to dinner?"

* * *

"I was so nervous to meet your parents," Anna said as she and Ethan stood outside the small farmhouse waiting for Anna's parents to arrive. "You look cool and collected."

"Well, I already know they're wonderful people, because they raised you, so I doubt they'd be unreasonable enough to rattle my nerves," he said with a laugh.

"You've been hanging around John too much," she said with a giggle. "You're becoming as silly as he is."

"Hey, John's a really good guy," Ethan said.

"I know. I'm kidding," she said, and gave him a peck on the cheek. "Oh, here they are!" she said as a sedan pulled into the driveway. She ran to greet them, waving and laughing as Ethan followed her.

Hugs and greetings followed, then she introduced Ethan. Turning to Ethan, she said, "These are my parents, Ellen and Ron."

The men shook hands and Ellen gave Ethan a hug. "It's so wonderful to meet you dear," Ellen said.

"Likewise," Ethan smiled.

"You've done a lot with the place," Ron said.

"You have no idea, Dad," Anna said with a laugh. "Well, no sense in wasting time, come on inside."

Her parents followed Anna and Ethan inside and looked around the farmhouse. "It's so charming," Ellen said.

"Come on," Anna said, leading them all to the elevator room. "Hang on, Mom and Dad," she said with a smile.

CHAPTER FORTY

When the elevator opened to the waterfall lobby, Ron and Ellen Shelby gasped in amazement.

"What is this place?" Ron asked.

"It's hard to explain until you've seen more of it," Anna said.

Ethan took the lead, showing Anna's parents the different parts of the underground mansion. The couple walked around wide-eyed and stunned, looking like they wouldn't even be able to walk on their own had they not been latched arm-in-arm on either side of their daughter.

They walked through the communal living and dining areas, the lounge, the gym and pool room, the gaming center, and finally headed into the communications room.

There, most of the team had finished work for the day, but Ethan showed Anna's parents a few of the projects they were working on at the workstations.

"So, Mom and Dad, Ethan built this whole thing as a sort of compound where he and the team could do the best charity work that would make the most difference in the world," explained Anna.

Finally, Ron Shelby spoke. "This is just… overwhelming. Incredible. I just can't think of enough words to describe it," he said.

"It's amazing," was all Ellen was able to verbalize.

"I have one more room to show you," said Anna. She led them across the hall to her office. "This is my office. I'm part of the team now! Vice President of Project Management," she said proudly.

"That's wonderful, dear," said Ron.

"That's fantastic. But are you giving up teaching?" asked her mother. Ellen Shelby had always been proud of the fact that her daughter was a teacher, just like her own mother had been.

"I haven't decided yet," said Anna. "But I am working on a project for a new school in South America for kids who otherwise wouldn't have access to a formal education. I'm working on the curriculum with a group of other teachers from around the world," she explained.

"Well, that's wonderful," said her mother.

"I'm still considering teaching, Mom, at least part time. But I haven't decided yet on any of it. It's all been so sudden," Anna said.

"This whole thing is so sudden," Ron said. "We're just trying to take it all in."

"I know, Dad," Anna said. "It was quite a shock to me, too."

"Why don't we go back to the lounge to relax and have some drinks before dinner?" Ethan suggested.

"That sounds lovely." Ellen smiled and nodded.

The group made their way back to the lounge, and Anna flashed Ethan a smile as he walked behind the bar. "What would everyone like?" he asked.

Everyone ordered the drinks they wanted, and Ethan expertly crafted each one, then joined the group at a nearby table. They spent the next hour talking about the underground mansion, how it was built, the people who worked there, and Ethan's reasons why he kept the charitable business so secretive.

"I wish I could, but I can't help everyone. Meeting face-to-face with so many more people than I could help really took a toll on my emotions. Also, it was impossible to do the research on whether one cause was worthy without a coordinated effort. So, here we are," Ethan explained.

"It's a wonderful place, Ethan," Ellen said. "And Anna, I'm so proud of you for being a part of it."

"Thanks, Mom," Anna said.

A member of the culinary team ducked his head into the room to say that dinner was ready.

"Thanks, Tim," Ethan said. "Well, dinner is served. Let's go see what Chef Benjamin created tonight!"

"I can't wait for this," Ron said.

"He's always excited about a new adventure in food," Ellen said with a giggle, and everyone laughed and talked all the way to the dining room, where the smell of garlic bread wafted through the air. Chef Benjamin had prepared his special lasagna recipe, along with homemade artisan breads and colorful fruit trays and garden salads.

"Our chef is Italian," Ethan explained as they ate, "and he always makes the most incredible authentic Italian dishes."

"I think Ron is in heaven," Ellen laughed.

Ron Shelby was closing his eyes and savoring the taste of each bite. "Delicious!" he exclaimed. "I'm coming here every night," he laughed.

"You're more than welcome to," Ethan said with a smile.

Dessert was a homemade strawberry gelato, which proved to be the perfect accompaniment to the meal.

"This is delicious," said Ellen. "But I ate so much lasagna, I don't think I can finish it."

As if on cue, Ron Shelby took the dish out of her hands and finished it up himself.

They all laughed.

The night wore on, and the group had lively conversations about the people and places of Belleville.

"Once I was out at Carroll Lake…" Ron began.

"Ron, you are not telling that one again," Ellen interrupted.

"Why not? It's a beautiful story." Ron folded his arms across his chest.

"It's about a fish," Ellen said.

"It was a really big fish."

"You didn't even catch it," Ellen said, then turned to Ethan. "He's about to tell you a fish story about a big fish that got away. He tells this story to everyone," she explained.

Ethan laughed. "It's okay. I'd love to hear it."

"So," continued Ron, "I was out at Carroll Lake, and we'd been fishing all afternoon. I think it was Rick, and Henry, and I think James. No, James was visiting his grandkids down in Texas around that time. So it must have been Ralph."

"Oh, for goodness sake, Ron, just tell the story and get it over with," Ellen said.

"So it was starting to get dark but we cast out anyway, and we could see in the water that there was this huge fish. The lake out there is just crystal clear. Out there in Carroll Lake," Ron continued.

Ellen shook her head and laughed.

"So I caught something, and it was big. We were sure it was that big fish we'd seen. So we pull up the line and lo and behold...." he paused for a moment for dramatic effect. "It was a shoe. A big, huge boot."

Everyone laughed.

The conversation continued for a while, then eventually Ellen and Ron rose to leave.

"I made those drinks a little strong," Ethan said. "Let me have someone drive you home. Someone can drive your car home, and we'll have another follow you to bring him back."

"That's probably a good idea," Ron looked as if his eyes were about to close.

Ethan texted some team members until he found two who were available. The group said their goodbyes outside, and Ron and Ellen Shelby were driven home.

Anna turned to Ethan. "That was wonderful. Thank you," she said, wrapping her arms around him.

"It was my pleasure. I had a great time," Ethan said.

They kissed under the stars, then held each other for a while as they gazed at the expanse of the country night sky.

"I know how we can keep having a great time." Anna gave him a sexy look.

Ethan raised his eyebrows, and Anna led him inside.

CHAPTER FORTY-ONE

Instead of heading for the elevator, Ethan led Anna by the hand to
the back bedroom of the charming country farmhouse.

"Let's sleep here," he said.

"Oh, we're going to sleep?" laughed Anna.

He led her to the bed and took her in his arms as they sat down. As
they kissed, he spun her around gently until he was on top of her,
caressing her hips and pulling her toward him.

"I love you, Anna Shelby," he said.

"I love you, Ethan Greenfield," Anna said in between kisses.

This time they undressed themselves, eager to get the clothes out
of the way quickly. Once joined as one, they pressed into each other
with slightly more force than they had before, each moaning with
pleasure as they reached their climax together.

They stayed fixed in each other's arms, drips of sweat melting into
one another as a cool breeze blew through an open window. For
several minutes, they laid together without a word, the only sound
being the gentle rhythm of crickets in the country night.

"That was wonderful," Anna said finally, rolling back slightly and
laying her head on Ethan's chest.

"Yes, it was," Ethan agreed, cradling her face and lifting it up as their lips met gently, then Anna put her head back on Ethan to listen to his heartbeat.

"I love this little farmhouse," she said.

"Yes, so do I. And my grandparents loved it, too, but living in the country just didn't work for my parents, so they never stayed here," he said.

"Not even once?" she asked.

"Maybe once or twice before I was born. I'm really not sure, but I can't picture my dad out in the country at all," he said.

"Neither can I," Anna said. "Of course, I've only seen him once, at the event, so I can't even picture him in anything but formalwear," she added with a laugh.

"He's rarely dressed casually," Ethan said. "When I was a kid, he'd always come downstairs already dressed in his business suit. He woke up really early and worked really hard. Well, I guess he would have done well with a farmer's schedule anyway," he said with a smile.

"Yes, he would," Anna said.

"Tell me something," Ethan said suddenly.

"About what?" Anna asked as she raised her head to look in his eyes.

"Anything. Everything. I want to know your hopes and dreams, your thoughts," he said.

"Okay," she said, moving back to lay her head on the pillow.

"Tell me about the animal shelter you want to open," he said. "Describe it. What would it look like?"

"Well, it wouldn't just be cages," she began. "That I know for sure. The areas would be big, and they'd open to the outside so the cats and dogs could get some fresh air whenever they wanted. Inside, they'd look more like homes than cages, with actual furniture. There'd be big areas where those who get along could be together, especially if they were surrendered from the same home. There would be a place where the shy and scared ones, and the ones who need medical attention, could feel safe and acclimate better to people so they have a chance at being adopted into a family."

"That sounds perfect," he said. "You've really thought this through."

"Only for my entire life," she said with a laugh. "And I'd find volunteers. Kids who love animals, and seniors who need to have a purpose in their days--they could come and just pet the animals and show them that people are good."

He turned to face her and propped up on his elbow with a big grin on his face.

"What?" she asked, studying his face to try to guess his thoughts.

"I have an idea. I've been thinking about it for a while," he said.

"What's that?" she asked, propping herself up so their faces were close.

"There's a property for sale next door with plenty of acreage. If I bought it, what would you think about building your shelter right there?" he asked.

"Really?" she said, sitting straight up in bed, the sheets falling off her.

Ethan looked at her body and gave her a quick, lustful smile, then turned serious. "Yes, really. I've been thinking of it for some time now, since I heard it was for sale."

"We can do that?" she said, getting more excited about the idea the more she thought about it.

"Yes. It's a charity that fits perfectly in our mission. This area is underserved on animal rescue since it's so rural. We could offer a new service to the county."

"Wait," she said. "Wouldn't that draw even more attention over here to the mansion? There would be more people coming and going."

"Not if we design it right. We're talking acres and acres here. We'd design it so the public enters on the opposite side of the acreage, and we'd leave a lot of the natural shrubbery between so that people wouldn't see any of what's happening over here. If anything, it would help explain the traffic more when we switch shifts," Ethan said.

"Ethan, it's such a wonderful idea!" she exclaimed, cradling his face in her hands and giving him a long and passionate kiss.

"I'm going to have to think of ideas like this more often," he joked.

They laughed, then kissed again and laid back down into more lovemaking.

* * *

ALL OF ETHAN'S CONNECTIONS MADE THE PROPERTY PURCHASE GO quickly. Ever since the night Ethan had suggested building the shelter, Anna had felt a new sense of energy and purpose. She dove into the project, working with an architect to design plans, connecting with experienced shelter operators, and meeting with animal welfare organizations to learn everything she needed to know to make the operation a success. She hired the best people to get the organization off the ground, using the team's contacts to find women and men who were just as excited about the project as she was, and just as committed to its success.

Eventually, she came to realize that living this dream meant she would have to leave her teaching career behind, at least for now. She put in her notice at the school and was happy to hear that some new younger teachers had been waiting for positions. Moving on to her own new opportunity would open up doors for others, and Anna felt proud of that. She would miss her students, but she was sure she would see most of them as volunteers at the shelter.

It wasn't long before construction began on the new shelter, and Anna spent most of her time readying her team for their new roles, which meant more time at the mansion. Several of the new team members were family or friends of existing team members, so they were also told about the mansion and its mission if they didn't already know. Everyone was proud to be a part of the effort.

One day, Anna walked into Ethan's office.

He looked up and smiled. "Hello there, beautiful," he said. "Need something?"

"Yes," she said. "I need to move in."

CHAPTER FORTY-TWO

Ethan got up from his desk and practically ran over to Anna. "Move in?" he asked excitedly.

"Yes," she said, then gave him a kiss. "I'm moving forward with my life, and it's all about the animal shelter and my work here... and you, of course."

"I couldn't be happier. I love you, Anna," he said, gazing into her emerald eyes.

"I love you, too," she said, wrapping her arms around him. Time stood still as they embraced tightly, their hearts beating in simultaneous rhythm as they basked in a feeling of contentment.

"We have a lot to do," he said after a while.

"Yes," she agreed. "I don't want to leave my house empty, so I think I'll ask if any of the new teachers need a place to stay."

"That's a great idea," he said.

"I need to plan!" she said excitedly. "So I'll see you tonight."

"No lunch?" he asked.

"Oh, I forgot to tell you. I'm having lunch with my parents. I need to talk to them about not teaching anymore. Do you want to come?"

"No, Anna. I know how much your mom loves that you're a

teacher, so I think that's a conversation you should have alone with them. I'll get something to eat here," he said.

"You're right. And thank you. You're wonderful!" she practically sang, leaning in for one more kiss before heading over to her office to make moving arrangements.

As Ethan had suggested, she had filled her office with her own decorative tastes, slowly bringing a few of her favorite things from her house. The room came to life with an assortment of her favorite houseplants, which she cared for with a loving touch.

"I'll bring Sammy first," she said to herself, then began contacting a moving company to start to arrange to have the rest of her things moved.

* * *

ANNA WAS ALREADY SEATED AT A TABLE WHEN HER PARENTS ARRIVED AT the restaurant. It was one of only two restaurants in the small town of Belleville, and everyone in town either ate there or ordered takeout from the Carrie's Diner menu. The local bakery also had a dining area and was usually open for lunch with a menu of sandwiches on fresh-baked bread. Anna chose Carrie's instead, since she knew how much her father loved their enchilada special.

She rose to her feet, greeting both of her parents with hugs before they sat down.

"You look so happy, dear," said her mother. "I'm so glad you found Ethan to share your life with."

"So am I," Anna said.

Linda looked over at her husband, who was already carefully examining the menu. "You know you're getting the enchiladas, dear. I don't know why you bother looking at the menu."

"I might want dessert," said Ron with a smile. His wife simply shook her head and looked back at Anna.

"So, dear, I know we're not just here for food," Linda said. "Do you have some news for us?" She raised her eyebrows after the question.

"It's not that… yet," Anna said with a smile. "Or that," she added, after watching her mother's expression.

Upon hearing that, Linda curled down her mouth slightly with disappointment.

"But it will come eventually, I'm sure. We're just both so busy right now with the shelter coming up, and of course Ethan has all of his projects," she explained.

"Okay," said Linda. "I'll let it slide for now. But I don't want to wait too long to watch you walk down the aisle… not to mention welcoming some grandchildren."

Anna felt her face flush slightly at the mention of a possible future pregnancy. "Someday, Mom. But I need to talk to you about my career choice right now," she said.

"You're leaving the school," Linda guessed.

"Yes. I love my students there, but the animal shelter has always been my dream," Anna said.

"We know that, dear," Linda said, "and your father and I support everything you're doing. You had your time as a teacher, and you did well. The experience will now color your entire future, because you'll always see things from a teacher's eyes."

"That's true," Anna agreed. "The experience has changed me for the better. Maybe someday I'll teach again. But for now, following through on this dream is what I want to do. What do you think, Dad?"

The question caught Ron Shelby off-guard, since he was already busy nibbling on the chips and salsa that the server had put on the table. "I want you to do what makes you happy, sweetheart," he said.

"Thank you, Dad," Anna said with a smile.

Their food arrived, and her father dug into his plate immediately. "You're just like a little kid when it comes to food, Ron," his wife said.

"I just appreciate a fine culinary effort," Ron said, and they all started laughing.

They enjoyed the rest of their meal, reminiscing about Anna's childhood and discussing the shelter construction. In the busy restaurant, they were careful not to mention the mansion at all, but everyone in town already knew that Anna was a part of the new animal shelter.

Over the past week, a couple of people in town had asked her about how it was financed, since it was a huge construction project by Belleville standards. When questioned, Anna just vaguely answered that she had some investors, and no one ever inquired further.

As they finished their meals, Anna's parents also had some polite conversations with some of the other people eating in the restaurant at nearby tables. In such a small town, no one ever passed up saying hello to a neighbor.

When Anna started to pay the check, her father protested for a moment, but she insisted. "This is my treat, Dad," she said.

Eventually, she hugged her parents goodbye and drove off to her house to get Sammy. He protested about going into the carrier, and Anna coaxed him in with a couple of treats.

"You're going to feel silly raising this much fuss," she told her cat. "You're going to love your new place! I think you'll love Milo, too."

She grabbed a few of her things that she wanted right away and loaded them into her car. The movers would be arriving in a few days, so she would come back the next day to pack everything else. She planned to leave behind a lot of her furniture, but Sammy's favorite chair would be clearly marked with some red tape to indicate that the movers should bring it along.

Anna lingered for a few minutes before she got in her car, looking at her home. She'd worked hard to buy it, and it would always be her own. But since someone else would be living there soon, she knew that after these next few days, it would be a while before she saw the inside of it again. She was thrilled with her life, with Ethan, and with her new job and the animal shelter, but despite all her happiness, she couldn't help but let a small tear escape as she got into her car to leave.

Sammy was next to her in the passenger's seat, complaining loudly about being cramped in the cat carrier. "We'll be home soon," she told him, and the thought of her new home put a smile back on her face.

As she exited her driveway, a brown car was parked a little way down the street, but Anna didn't notice it. Sitting inside was a man with short sandy hair and blue eyes. When Anna pulled away, he started his car and followed her.

CHAPTER FORTY-THREE

About a week later, Anna was starting to settle in. She'd taken one of the rooms in the mansion as her own, although she shared Ethan's bed every night. She had so many things that she didn't want to give away, so she used them to decorate a room as a quiet place she could go when she wanted to unwind. She also put Sammy's favorite chair in the room so he could feel more comfortable, although he loved the pets' room and was already warming up to Milo.

Kelly helped her decorate. "This stuff looks even better in this room," she laughed.

"That's true," Anna agreed.

"When do I get to be a maid of honor?" Kelly asked, raising her eyebrows at her friend.

"I'm sure that'll come soon enough. We're so busy with everything, it's hard to even have much time together," Anna explained.

"Well, make time," Kelly said bluntly. "There's more to living here than building an animal shelter or working with the team. You need to take time to communicate so your relationship grows."

"You're right," Anna said. "We do try to make as much time as we can. Once things are running smoothly, maybe we'll go on a vacation."

"That'd be nice. LA again?" Kelly asked.

"Oh, I don't know. I mean, I'd love to see his parents again. But I'd like to go someplace more romantic."

"You should go somewhere tropical, a secluded island," Kelly suggested.

"Maybe. Or maybe somewhere overseas. I don't know. We'll figure it out later," she laughed.

* * *

Later that night, Ethan and Anna were having dinner in the mansion's dining room with Kelly and John.

"A toast," Ethan said, "to my best mechanic ever."

"Thank you, thank you," said John, rising from his chair. "I'd just like to thank my beautiful Kelly, for making all this possible."

"I…," began Kelly.

"But I can't forget the little people, who also helped along the way. It all began in an old, rustic hospital far away from civilization…," John said.

"You were born in Bluewater," Kelly interrupted, rolling her eyes. "And Bluewater General was a brand-new hospital back then."

"Well, if it was new, maybe they didn't know how to use all the equipment," he added. "So my entrance into the world was truly brave."

"You're a goof," Kelly said.

Suddenly Ethan's phone rang. "Excuse me," he said before answering.

"You'd better get down here," Rick said on the other end of the line. "The alarm's going off."

"Be right there," Ethan said as he rose. Anna looked at him quizzically. "We have an alarm," he explained.

"Alarm?" Anna said with a furrowed brow. Sudden panic overcame her, and her entire body started trembling. She'd had a strange feeling ever since coming back home from LA, as if someone was watching her. "What if it's Alan?" she said with alarm.

"It can't be," Kelly said. "He's gone for good."

"I don't know that," Anna said, then she rose to follow Ethan. "I'm going with you."

"So are we." John and Kelly followed Ethan and Anna to the security room.

"We've got someone out there, and he's yelling," said Rick when they arrived in the room. He pointed to a security camera, where a man could be seen by the garage entrance barn pacing and yelling incoherently, something about revealing the secret.

Anna breathed a sigh of relief when she saw that it wasn't Alan. "Do we know that man?" she asked.

"He looks familiar," Ethan said. "I'm going up."

"I'm going with you," John and Rick said simultaneously. Rick grabbed the weapons and gave one each to Ethan and John.

"Please be careful." Anna gave him a worried look..

Ethan gave her a quick kiss. "Don't worry. It'll be fine," he said.

Kelly and Anna stayed in the security room and watched the camera feed. They saw the men exit the barn and confront the man, who yelled at all of them. Despite being verbally confrontational, the man seemed to back away somewhat. Finally, he put his head down, dropped a piece of paper, and said something to Ethan that the women couldn't hear on the camera feed. The man then walked to a car out front, got in, and drove away. Ethan, John, and Rick returned to the security room soon after.

"Who was that?" Anna asked.

"He's an old business rival of mine from LA. His name is David Browning. He and his family have a rival development company that competes with my family's business. How he got here or found out about all this, I have no idea," said Ethan. "He was going on about revealing our secret."

"Should we worry about him?" Kelly asked.

"We probably don't need to worry too much, but we do need to deal with him," Ethan said. "He left his number on a piece of paper, so I'll call him tomorrow and figure out how to work this out."

"Do you think he'll do something tonight?" Anna asked.

"It's not likely. He left his number for a reason. He needs to talk to me, and he knows I won't ever talk to him if he goes around making good on those threats," Ethan said.

"It's still unnerving." Anna turned to Kelly. "Do you want to stay here tonight?"

Kelly looked at John. "I'd like to go home and make sure everything's fine there. I'm sure he's not after me or John specifically, but I'll feel better knowing everything is okay at home."

Anna gave her and John hugs. "Be careful, please. I'm sure it's nothing, but I want you both safe."

"We'll be fine," John assured her, and he and Kelly left for home.

* * *

LATER THAT NIGHT, ANNA HAD TROUBLE GETTING TO SLEEP. SHE AND Ethan were in Ethan's suite, and even cuddled in his arms she felt nervous.

"What do you think he wants?" she asked.

"I don't know, but I'll find out first thing in the morning. I'm sure it's nothing you need to worry about," he said.

"How will you handle him?" Anna asked.

"I know David pretty well. We pretty much grew up together. Maybe he was drunk tonight or something because he usually doesn't act like that. I think I can reason with him once he's sobered up, or calmed down a little," Ethan said.

"I hope so. I don't know him, but I tend to agree. He looked more hurt than angry, from what I could tell on the video screen," she said.

"Yeah. I got that general idea, too," he said. "I'll call him tomorrow. Whatever he wants, I could pay him off like I did with Alan, but I don't think that works in most cases. He will just want more. I mean, it's okay to do to get someone like Alan out of our lives, and with him, I know it's pure greed, so it'll work. But with David, I think I just need to hear him out and listen to what he wants. I don't want you to worry, Anna. We'll get this straightened out."

"I know we will. I'm just glad it wasn't Alan. I don't know how I would have handled that," she said.

"Neither do I, really. But that's not the case, so we don't have to worry about that."

"You're right," Anna said as she snuggled up closer and felt the beat of Ethan's heart on her cheek.

CHAPTER FORTY-FOUR

Ethan called David early that next morning. He wanted to get the problem taken care of right away so that Anna didn't have to keep worrying. She had a lot on her mind planning the construction and opening for the animal shelter, and she was still working on the team's educational projects. All that was a lot on her plate, and she didn't need to have some drunk old business partner to worry about on top of it all.

"We need to talk," he told David on the phone.

"Yes, we do," David said.

"Let's meet in Bluewater. Name the place," Ethan said.

"Delany's Café. It's over on Melvin Street," he said.

"Alright," Ethan said. "I'll be there at noon."

* * *

Delany's was a rustic place. It was clear the owner wasn't too worried about decorating, but the food was good. Ethan and Rick had gone there many times when planning the mansion's construction.

Ethan walked in the door and saw David already sitting in a booth. He slid into the seat on the other side.

"So why don't you tell me why you were screaming at my barn in the middle of the night," he said, without saying hello first. David and Ethan had grown up together, and even though their families had competitive businesses, the kids felt more like brothers than rivals. At least that's how it was when they were kids. That made small pleasantries mostly unnecessary, especially since Ethan was upset about how scared David had made Anna feel.

"It all kind of came to a head in my mind," David said.

"Care to elaborate?" Ethan said.

"I saw you back in LA that weekend, the one with the gala. At first I tried to ignore you, but I kept seeing you at all these ritzy places, the billionaire with all the chicks, the cars, and the fancy clothes. It just sort of set off something in my head," David said.

"Go on." Ethan leaned back in his seat. The server came by, and he ordered a coffee.

"Business has been pretty bad at Browning, Inc.," explained David. "It's because Dad won't ever listen to anything I say. So we lost a lot of business and our profits are way down. It's expensive living in LA, so we can't go out to fancy galas and hang around with beautiful chicks like you can."

"First of all," Ethan said. "Anna is no 'chick,' just to get that cleared up right now."

"Sorry. You know what I mean," David said.

"So what won't he listen to you about?" Ethan asked.

"He's focused on all these high-end buildings that cost a fortune to build and don't sell the units at a decent profit. Plus, he invested in all these malls. No one goes to malls anymore, especially the ones he picked. It's like anything Dad puts his money into just goes downhill. I'm kind of worried about him, really," David said.

"He's always had a hard head. My dad wanted to go into business with him back in the day. He wouldn't listen to him, either. Always wanted to do things his own way. His pride has kept him from succeeding most of his life," Ethan said.

"Exactly. So when I found out about you and your secret underground mansion and all that, I just couldn't stand it anymore. I followed you out here, and I'm afraid I had a lot to drink last night. I was trying to get up the nerve to confront you," he said.

"About what?" Ethan asked. "And how in the world did you know where I am or what I'm doing?"

"Honestly, I don't know what I was gonna confront you on. I just wanted to holler at you really. As to the mansion, remember that we have a lot of contacts in common. Remember Joe Selma?"

"Joe told you?" Ethan asked. It was hard to imagine that Joe Selma, who helped the team with the project in South America, would tell anyone about the mansion. Joe had worked on the team for a few years, and Ethan thought of him as a friend.

"No, no. It's not his fault," Ethan explained. "I tricked him. Acted like I already knew all about it and that I had worked for you. I pieced together clues from some of the things he said. Talked his ear off. It wasn't easy, but I figured it out."

"If you did, I'm sure others will figure it out soon enough," Ethan said.

"I don't think so. The person would have to know you just as well as I do, plus they'd have to have a trusting relationship with Joe. The guy is a saint. It's not his fault," David said.

"All the same, I'll talk to him," Ethan said.

"Go easy on him. I was tricked." David laughed.

"You can be sneaky, I'll give you that," Ethan said. "But what do you want? I mean, there's nothing I can do about your Dad. He's already set in his ways and wouldn't listen to a Greenfield to save his life."

"I really don't know what I wanted. I was just so pissed. At him, at myself, at the world. You seemed like a good target to take it out on." David chuckled.

"Well, you worried the heck out of my girlfriend, and she didn't deserve that," Ethan said firmly.

"I know, and I'm sorry," David said. "She sure is a beauty."

"Yes, she is. Beauty with brains and scruples, the whole package," Ethan said.

"You always get the best of everything," David said. "But I think I can be happy for you. You seem happy. You were never so happy as a kid."

"David, what happened to us? We used to be friends as kids," Ethan said.

"I don't know. Our parents, I guess. I mean, probably my dad really. He got so mad whenever I said anything about you. He didn't want you to be my friend," David explained.

Ethan sat back and sipped his coffee for a few minutes. "Well," he said. "There's really only one solution to our problem here."

"What's that?" David asked.

"I need to hire you," Ethan replied.

* * *

Months passed by quickly, and it seemed like no time had passed until construction was done on the animal shelter, and it was time to open its doors to the community's homeless animals. Anna quickly busied herself with finding all the animals who needed her help.

In all that time, David had shown to be a valuable member of the team. Ethan had hired him as a project manager and put him to work on development projects. He had a great eye for successful ventures and became more confident now that he no longer worked for his father. Browning, Inc., went on without him, but was never a very successful business.

Despite the difficult way they were introduced, Anna liked working with David. As the Vice President of Project Management, Anna worked with David all the time, and they had a good working relationship.

* * *

Everyone was finishing up for the day one evening when Ethan walked into Anna's office.

"Things seem pretty settled," he told her. "We've rescued lots of cats and dogs and have lots of volunteers. The teams are all working on the projects, and I think they have everything handled for now. I think it's time for you and me to take a little vacation. What do you say?"

"Vacation!" exclaimed Anna. "You know that sounds wonderful. Where will we go?"

"I'm thinking Paris," he said.

CHAPTER FORTY-FIVE

"Paris!?" Anna exclaimed after Ethan had suggested the trip.

"Yes, Paris. Have you ever been there?" Ethan asked.

"No. No, I haven't. Oh, my goodness, Paris! When would we leave?" she said, pacing around the office. She spied the files on her desk and spoke before Ethan could answer her. "But I have so much to do. We have so much to do. Do you think we can really get away?"

"That's why we have a team, Anna." Ethan smiled. "While your work is valuable, it's okay to take a vacation once in a while. And you've been going non-stop since the shelter construction started."

"I guess that's true," Anna admitted. "I'll need some time to get my team up to speed, though."

"As will I," he said. "We're not leaving tomorrow." He laughed, and she joined in.

"When should we go?" she asked.

"We'll give it two weeks. That should be plenty of time to get everyone in place to cover us while we're gone. Is your passport up to date?" he asked.

"I don't know. I mean, I've never been out of the country before," she said. "But I did get a passport once, just in case. I had dreams of flying all over the world, so I thought I'd better have one." She giggled, and he came closer and gave her a kiss.

"Well, I'm glad you did that. We'll have to check the expiration. But it's easier to renew than to get one for the first time," he said.

"It must be in this stuff," she said, going to her filing cabinet. "I keep all my important papers here."

"Hopefully it's up to date, then we can leave in two weeks," he said.

"Yes, here we go. Yay! I have a year left!" she said, practically jumping up and down with excitement.

"That's wonderful," said Ethan. "I'll go make the arrangements. Let's plan on two weeks from today. Sound good?"

"Oh, that sounds amazing!" she exclaimed. "Oh, I've got to tell Kelly!"

"I'll go get everything started," he said. She practically ran over to him and wrapped her arms around him, then gave him a passionate kiss.

"You're so wonderful," she said.

"I love you, Anna. We need some special time together," he said.

"I agree," said Anna.

"I'll meet you in the dining room in about an hour," said Ethan.

They kissed once more, then Ethan went to his office to call his travel agent. Anna ran back to her desk and called Kelly.

"I'm going to Paris!" she squealed.

"Oh, my goodness, Anna. That's fantastic!" exclaimed Kelly. "When do you leave?"

"In two weeks. We'll need to make arrangements to cover all our work. Can you help?"

"Of course I can! Just let me know what you need me to do," said Kelly.

"I've got some files on my desk that I can go over with you, if you have some time tomorrow," said Anna.

"Yes, I'll be there in the morning. I'm so excited for you, Anna! You two deserve a fun, romantic trip!" Kelly said.

"We haven't had time to really spend together doing fun things," Anna said. "I wish you and John could come."

"This trip is just for the two of you. We'll plan on a double date trip some other day. Although I'm not sure Europe is ready for John!" she laughed.

"We'd definitely have to supervise him!" Anna laughed.

"Have you told your parents yet?" Kelly asked.

"Nope, that's my next phone call. You were first," Anna said.

"Hooray! I love getting all the best news first," Kelly said.

They chatted a bit more, then Anna called her parents, who were happy for the news.

"We can certainly help out in the shelter if you need us," her mother said.

"That would be great! I'll let Kelly know everything going on, and she can show you what to do," Anna said.

With plans made to cover all the work she'd miss while in Paris, Anna closed up her office and went to the dining room.

* * *

"This is going to be such a long plane trip," Anna said as they boarded Ethan's private jet weeks later. "I've never been in the air for that long."

"It's no different from the trip to LA. Just think of it as more time for snacks and movies," Ethan said with a laugh.

Anna had spent the past week shopping for new clothes to wear on their trip. She had no idea what the styles were in Europe, but a helpful fashion consultant at a boutique in Bluewater had helped her choose some fashion-forward looks.

She was so excited about her destination. She'd never been anywhere outside of the US before, and even within the States, she'd only visited a few places. She felt comfortable knowing that Ethan had been to Paris before, so he'd be able to show her the sights.

It was quite a long trip, and eventually she was able to calm her excitement enough to take a couple of naps. The comfortable furnishings in Ethan's private jet made it easy to relax.

It was dark when they finally landed, and as they drove through

215

the city to their hotel, Anna was stunned by the exquisite architecture, every building intricately designed with Parisian charm. Their hotel was no exception, and Anna gazed up at it in awe as Ethan talked to the baggage handlers.

After everything was sorted, he took Anna's hand and led her inside their hotel.

CHAPTER FORTY-SIX

Ethan and Anna's Parisian hotel room was stunning, decorated in shades of blue with grand curtains draped behind the bed and over the windows. A huge set of French doors opened to a large, splendid veranda with a view of the lit-up Eiffel Tower.

"I can't believe we're here!" exclaimed Anna, running toward the terrace to get a look of the city. Ethan tipped the baggage handlers and walked up behind her, wrapping his arm around her waist. She gazed up at him. "I love you so much! Thank you for this trip. This is amazing!" she told him.

He faced her and caressed her cheek. "I would do anything for you," he said. "It's late, but we can probably order room service if you're hungry."

"I am a little, yes," she said. "Maybe just a light snack, not a full dinner."

Ethan called the concierge and arranged for a meal while Anna started to unpack. They would be in the city for two weeks, and she wanted to wear all of her new outfits. It wasn't long before there was a knock on the door.

Room service had arrived. It was a bread and cheese platter, with authentic homemade baguettes and an assortment of fine French cheeses.

"This is delicious," Anna said.

"I have so many restaurants to take you to. You'll never eat quite as well as you do in Paris. Everything is a culinary delight," Ethan said.

They ate while going through some brochures Ethan had brought from his previous trips in Paris, planning all the places they would visit during their trip.

"I wish there was more time to see them all," she said.

"We'll do a great general tour this time," explained Ethan. "Then next time we come, we'll try the things that we didn't get to this round. There will be plenty of time for more trips to Paris."

"You're so wonderful," she said.

"We'd better get to sleep early," he said, "so we can start first thing in the morning. There's nothing quite like Paris on a summer morning."

"I can't wait to sleep in that bed. It looks simply luxurious," she said as they finished up their snack.

"I can tell you that it is," he said. "I usually choose this hotel when I can get in."

He took her by the hand and pulled her gently toward him. He brushed a strand of hair away from her eyes and felt her cheek with the tips of his fingers. Their lips met, gently at first, then with a deeper passion as their hands slid across each other's bodies. Slowly they moved, locked in their passionate embrace as he guided her onto the bed. He paused the kiss when they laid down, pulling away slightly to gaze into her eyes as he unbuttoned her blouse slowly. She reached up for his shirt, and he stopped with her buttons half undone to help her remove his own shirt, revealing the firm muscles of his chest. She started to reach for her own blouse, but he gently took her hand and interlocked their fingers.

"Let me do it," he said.

She nodded as he took his time on each button, kissing each inch of her exposed skin. He then moved his fingers to open her front-hook bra, moving his hands over her breasts slowly as he uncovered each one. They kissed again, then she rolled over on top of him, unbuttoning his pants and sliding them down until he kicked them off. He reached up her skirt and removed her panties but left the skirt in place as he entered her.

Something about the atmosphere in the room, the air itself in Paris, made Anna feel more daring, more confident, more lustful. Ethan followed her lead as she made love to him with a wild passion under the royal blue curtains.

* * *

"So much for an early start," laughed Anna the next morning as she kissed him. "But I wouldn't trade last night for anything."

"I agree," said Ethan. "That was incredible. And it'll take a few days to get used to the time change anyway. Then we can do some early morning sightseeing."

"That sounds wonderful," she said.

They got up and showered to get ready to go explore the city. Anna wore one of the sundresses she'd bought back in Bluewater, and Ethan changed into some lightweight slacks and a blue shirt that was nearly the color of his eyes.

It was lunchtime in Paris by the time they were out and about, so Ethan took her to a nearby restaurant for some authentic Parisian fare. Anna was impressed by the different flavors of the dishes.

"You won't get this in Belleville," she joked.

"There's something to be said for every local cuisine, and the Midwest has some great food," said Ethan. "Paris is just... extraordinary."

"That it is," she agreed.

For the next two weeks, they visited museums, theaters, and all the finest restaurants near their hotel as Ethan showed her all the sights of the city. Anna felt as though she were in a dream, in some magical place, a romantic kingdom with her very own prince, and she was the princess. It was easy to feel the magic of Paris; everywhere they were surrounded by the charm of the city.

On the morning of their last day, Ethan and Anna ate breakfast on the terrace overlooking the city.

"Tonight, we're going there," he said, pointing to the Eiffel Tower. "I saved the best for last."

"I can't wait!" she said.

They spent another day sightseeing and shopping, and Anna was sure to pick up souvenirs to take back to Kelly, John, and her parents. She even bought a dish for Sammy decorated with the sights of Paris.

That night, they walked up to the front of the Eiffel Tower, looking straight up at its majestic heights. It was lit up from top to bottom with thousands of shimmering white bulbs shining brightly in the city's skyline. When they reached a place near the center of the tower, Ethan stopped Anna and opened a pack he'd been carrying. He took out a compact chair and unfolded it, indicating to Anna that she should sit down. She did, then she looked straight up at the bright lights of the tower in awe.

When she looked back down, Ethan was down on one knee beside her.

"Anna, my love," he said. "Before I met you, I felt a void in my life. You came along like a miracle and filled it with love, hope, and happiness. My beautiful, wonderful Anna, would you be my wife, and fill my life with happiness forever?"

CHAPTER FORTY-SEVEN

"Yes, yes!" Anna exclaimed immediately after Ethan proposed, as he held a large and beautiful sparkling diamond ring in front of him. She dove down and met him on the ground with a hug, practically knocking him over. He set the ring down for a minute, because the immediate joy for both Anna and Ethan was their kiss--and the excitement of their future together.

"Let's not forget this," Ethan said after a few minutes. He took her hand in his and slid the ring on her finger.

"It's so beautiful!" she exclaimed. "Thank you."

They kissed once more, the sparkling lights of the Eiffel Tower glittering in the night sky above them.

* * *

As soon as they returned to their hotel room, Anna called Kelly. Her friend welcomed the news with more of a squeal than words at first, then she finally calmed her excitement.

"I knew he was going to propose in Paris! What better place for it?" Kelly said.

"I was hoping so, but I was happy just having a vacation together," Anna said. "Now, I'm just on top of the world!"

"Did you set a date?"

"Not yet. We have lots of plans to make. I hate to let you go, but I need to tell Mom and Dad," Anna said.

"Yes, call them right away. They're going to be so excited! We can talk more later." Kelly said. "I'm so happy for you, Anna."

"Thanks, Kelly. I'm pretty happy myself," Anna said.

They said their goodbyes, and the next call was to her parents.

"Finally!" Anna's mother exclaimed. "Oh, my dear, I'm so happy for you. Did you set a date?" Ellen asked.

"Not yet. We'll start making plans now, and I'll let you know soon," Anna said.

"I'm so happy, dear," her mother replied.

"Me, too, Mom." Anna smiled at her mother.

They talked for a few more minutes, then Anna hung up.

"Did you tell them?" she asked Ethan, who was walking in from the other room after making his own phone calls.

"Yes, my parents are thrilled, and Rick is excited about being best man," Ethan said with a smile.

"Oh, no! I forgot to ask Kelly to be my maid of honor," Anna said.

Ethan laughed. "I'm sure she knows that the job is all hers," he said.

"Yes, I'm sure she does. I'm so excited, Ethan. I can hardly wait to be Mrs. Greenfield!" she said.

"I can't wait, either," he said. "Anna, I've been looking for you all my life. I can't believe that I found you, and now you're going to be my wife. I love you so much."

"I love you too, Ethan," she said, and they leaned into each other for a passionate kiss.

Ethan and Anna spent their last night in Paris making love and beginning to make plans for their wedding--and their future.

* * *

ANNA COULDN'T NAP AT ALL ON THE PLANE RIDE HOME AS THEY discussed details about the wedding. They decided to have the ceremony at Anna's family's church in Belleville, where they could invite all of her friends, family, and former students. Most of Ethan's friends already worked in the mansion, so they could attend, and his parents would fly in for the ceremony. They would keep things quiet so that the media didn't overwhelm the occasion in the small town.

It was still nighttime back home during some of their flight, but as soon as it was morning in Belleville, Anna called the church and booked a date on a weekend six months from the current date. Anna and Ethan figured they would need that much time to plan all the details.

Having a firm date made Anna even more excited about the wedding, and she and Ethan spent the rest of the flight making lists of everything to think about for the big occasion.

* * *

ANNA, HER MOTHER, AND KELLY WERE OUT DRESS SHOPPING THE NEXT weekend. This was one item that Anna didn't want to wait to buy.

"There are too many," she said. "How am I ever going to decide? This is once in a lifetime, and I want it to be perfect."

"You'll know, dear," said her mother. "And Kelly and I will also know the second you walk out of that fitting room in it."

"I hope so," said Anna.

"She's right," said Kelly. "It's just going to be one of those things you automatically know is right."

"Like marrying Ethan," said Anna with a smile.

"Yes!" exclaimed her friend.

The color was the first choice for Anna, who wasn't sure if she wanted a bright white gown, ivory, or another unique color. The bridal boutique consultant helped by showing different fabric swatches against her to see how they looked with her coloring. It turned out that no color looked better than a pure, bright white against her reddish hair.

223

Style was the next choice.

"I've always wanted to wear a fairy princess gown, but I don't know if I'd like a full skirt," Anna said.

"I think you should get something form-fitting for that perfect figure of yours," Kelly said.

"I completely agree," Ellen said.

The bridal consultant smiled. "I have a few choices that I think you'd look wonderful in," she said. "I'll go get a few."

All the dresses looked the same on the hangers, but Anna discovered subtle differences as she tried each one on. Some had more coverage than others. Some had more lace detail. Others had more pearls or beads. And each of them had a slightly different shaping and train style. Anna liked them all.

'I'm never going to be able to choose,' she thought as she tried on gown after gown.

Finally, the consultant brought in a strapless mermaid-style dress with an elegantly laced, flowing train.

"Oh, my gosh," she said when she saw herself in the mirror after trying it on. "Mom! Kelly!" she called.

They came running back into the fitting room.

"Oh, my beautiful baby girl," her mother said as tears started welling up in her eyes.

"Anna," Kelly said. "I've never seen you look so happy and beautiful. That's the one!"

CHAPTER FORTY-EIGHT

THE FLOWERS, the cake, and catering--everything was falling into place sooner than Anna expected. Ethan had suggested hiring a wedding planner, but Anna wanted herself and Ethan to do most of the planning for their special day.

"I want our ceremony to be a part of us, to reflect our tastes completely," she had said.

"Wedding planners can do that," Ethan had said. "They make all the arrangements and do all the legwork, but they give you choices on all the colors and details."

"I know, but I want to do that all myself. I've dreamed of my wedding--our wedding--my entire life. It's only one day, but I can drag out the experience by doing all that legwork myself," she said. "Well, with some help from you," she added, grinning.

"Well, when you put it that way, I'm in!" he said with a smile.

Anna's father had made the grand sacrifice - as he described it - of being the official taster of the Ethan and Anna wedding. That included sampling all the different cake flavor options as well as all the dishes that the caterers proposed to serve.

"It makes me feel useful," Ron insisted one day, with a mouthful of food he was 'tasting.'

Ellen and Anna just shook their heads and laughed.

* * *

ONE MORNING, ETHAN ENTERED ANNA'S OFFICE WHILE SHE WAS working on the education project.

"How's your afternoon looking?" he asked.

"I'm getting these ideas ready for Cliff before lunchtime, so I was planning on heading to the shelter afterward. Why?" she asked.

"Oh, I just thought you might want to go shopping with me for the rings we plan to wear for the rest of our lives," he said with a sexy smile.

"Yes! I'd love to!" she exclaimed, jumping up and wrapping her arms around Ethan. "I'll ask Kelly if she can cover over there for the afternoon."

"I thought you'd say yes," he said.

"Now how am I supposed to concentrate until lunchtime?" she asked with a giggle.

"You'll make it through. I have to do some boring paperwork myself, so wish me luck on that," he laughed.

After Ethan left, it was hard to concentrate, but Anna refocused her mind by considering how important the new school would be for the children, and how much their parents would rely on her curriculum to help their children's future. She got back to work, energized with even more new ideas to make the school project a success. She ended up working a few minutes into the lunch hour to finish up, then took the file to Cliff and went to meet Ethan.

"Do you want to eat here or get a bite while we're out?" Ethan asked.

"Let's eat here first. Something smells delicious in the dining room, and I don't want to miss out," she said.

Chef Benjamin had prepared an incredible pasta dish and salad for lunch, and both Ethan and Anna enjoyed their meals while chatting with some of the team members in the dining room.

Soon after, they headed out, driving to Bluewater for ring shopping. There were no fine jewelry stores in Belleville or the surrounding towns.

"I'll take you to where I bought your engagement ring," Ethan said as he drove. "I know that normally, they just add a band to the engagement ring for the wedding, but for our wedding rings, I want you to choose something yourself. It's important that you love it."

"I love my engagement ring!" she exclaimed. "Although I wouldn't mind also having a different wedding ring. I've had something in mind since I was a little girl," she added.

"I thought you would have," he said. "I'd love to buy you the ring of your dreams, then you could wear your engagement ring on the other hand."

"I would love that. You're so wonderful," she said, giving him a kiss on the cheek as he drove down the highway toward Bluewater.

They arrived at the jewelry store, and Ethan held the door open as Anna entered. The jewelry cases were filled with beautiful, sparkling fine jewelry, and Anna and Ethan made their way straight to the wedding rings.

"Hello, Mr. Greenfield," the jewelry consultant greeted them.

"Hello, Edward. I'd like you to meet my beautiful bride, Anna," Ethan said.

"Hello." Anna smiled at the kind looking man.

"It's wonderful to meet you, Anna." Edward extended his hand, and she shook it. "I take it the proposal was a success, and we're ready for the second half of the ring."

"Actually, Edward," Ethan began, "we're going to have Anna choose a perfect ring herself."

"I understand completely," Edward replied, then he turned to Anna. "Have a seat over there, and I'll bring some of our finest collections for you to see."

"Thank you," she said as they walked over to sit down by a desk made of glass.

All the rings were beautiful, but Anna scanned each tray to find exactly the style she had been picturing since girlhood. After several trays, she was starting to think that her design was just something that a little girl would think up, but suddenly something caught her eye on the very next tray.

She picked it up. It was a stunning piece with a marquise-cut diamond, set with other small stones in such a way that they looked like lace, with intricate carvings in the white gold that would surround her finger.

"That's perfect," Ethan said, knowing by the look in Anna's eye that she'd found the style she loved.

"It is!" she exclaimed. "It's exactly how I always pictured it!"

"Then it's yours," he said.

Edward gave Ethan a nod. "It's an exquisite piece, very fine craftsmanship. That ring is one of a kind, created by a very talented designer in Paris."

"Paris!" Anna exclaimed. "How perfect!"

Edward looked at Ethan. "The same designer has a collection of men's wedding bands. Would you like to see them?"

"Of course," he said, and Edward had his assistant bring them out.

"Which should I choose?" Ethan asked Anna.

"This is your decision, Ethan," she said. "Just like mine is perfect for me, I want your ring to be perfect for you."

Ethan smiled and took a few minutes to look over the collection, but he kept coming back to the first one that had caught his eye. It was also white gold, just like Anna's ring, and was inlaid with several diamonds in a thick, solid band with carvings on either edge.

"I love it!" exclaimed Anna when Ethan made his selection.

"Excellent!" Edward exclaimed. "It looks like we won't need to do much sizing on either one, so let's take some measurements and we'll have them ready in no time."

* * *

TIME PASSED QUICKLY, AND SOON IT WAS ALMOST ETHAN AND ANNA'S wedding day.

CHAPTER FORTY-NINE

It was the night before Ethan and Anna's wedding, and Anna was spending the night at Kelly's house. She wanted to make her and Ethan's wedding night as special as she could, so she had decided that they wouldn't wake up in the same bed on the day of the wedding. Ethan had been very understanding.

"Sweetheart, I know how much this day has meant to you since you were a little girl. We have the rest of our lives to spend our nights together, so if it means our wedding will be perfect for you with one night apart, I'm on board," Ethan had told her.

She also wanted to be with her best friend on her special night. Kelly and Anna had grown up together, and it was with Kelly that Anna had shared all her hopes and dreams about her future wedding day.

"I'm so excited, and so nervous, all at the same time!" Anna confided in her friend.

"Because it's such an important day for you," said Kelly. "But you know I've got your back. Anything that needs to be done to make it perfect, I'll be there."

"I know you will," Anna said, hugging her friend.

"Now let's eat some snacks!" Kelly laughed. They had planned to spend the evening talking, watching movies, and eating all the snacks they loved as kids, just like one of their sleepovers from when they were younger.

"I honestly don't know if I can eat," Anna said.

"What's wrong? I've never known you to turn down popcorn," Kelly said, popping some kernels of the treat into her mouth.

Anna laughed. "I love popcorn, that's for sure. No, it's that my nerves have got my stomach in knots. What if I trip walking down the aisle? What if I forget what to say? What if Ethan changes his mind tonight and decides to just fly off in his jet and never come back?" Anna asked in a panic voice, pacing around the room.

"Whoa, Whoa, " Kelly said as she stood up and walked over to her friend. "Honey, breathe. That's it, deep breath, hold it… now exhale slowly. Okay, now another. Good girl." Kelly brought her hands up and down slowly to illustrate the pace Anna should breathe. "You're getting yourself in a panic, and you don't have to do that. First of all, that man will be waiting at the altar for you long before you've got your makeup ready."

Anna let out a nervous giggle.

"That's it. I'm hilariously funny, so you need to relax and laugh with me. If you trip, I'll catch you. And if you mess up your lines, it won't matter. The pastor will talk you through it. You'll be fine," Kelly said with a smile.

"I hope you're right," Anna said.

"Of course I am. I'm always right," Kelly said, and they both laughed again.

* * *

ETHAN'S PARENTS HAD FLOWN IN AND WERE STAYING IN A ROOM IN THE mansion. Ethan had just said goodnight to them and showed them to their room when he walked into the lounge. Normally it would have been empty this time of night, but Rick was there standing behind the bar.

"About time you got here," he said.

Ethan laughed. "You know me too well, old friend," he said.

"Who are you calling old?" Rick laughed.

"Well, you're older than me," Ethan said.

"Not by much. How are you holding up on your last night as an eligible bachelor?" Rick asked.

"I'm excited, and honestly a little nervous. I just hope I get the lines right."

"My friend, 'I do' is one of the shortest sentences in the English language," Rick laughed.

Ethan chuckled. "Sure," he said, "But we wrote our own vows. You know that."

"I know. I'm just kidding. You'll be fine. We've rehearsed them a thousand times."

"I'm a lucky man, marrying a woman like Anna," Ethan said.

"Yes, yes you are," Rick agreed. "And she's a lucky woman. You've been a good man all your life, Ethan, and you deserve this."

"I hope I can be a good husband to her," Ethan said, his eyes gazing out in the distance.

"You know you will be," Rick said, pouring Ethan a drink.

"I hope you're right, buddy," Ethan said.

"When am I ever wrong?" Rick laughed.

* * *

"Do I look okay, Mom?" Anna asked.

The stylist had finished her hair, which was shaped into a romantic messy updo with loose tendrils framing her face. In place of a traditional wedding veil, Anna had opted for a spray of ribbons and flowers that cascaded down one side, gently brushing her bare shoulder above her strapless wedding dress. The makeup artist had also just finished. Although Anna was a natural beauty, the artist had given her natural looking coverage and shaded her eyelids with the perfect hue to bring out the emerald jewel tones in her eyes.

"Honey, you look like a princess, like a goddess, like my beautiful baby girl on her wedding day." Her mother was having a difficult time keeping her own mascara from running since her eyes were almost constantly watering with tears of happiness.

"Mom, don't make me cry. I'll mess up my makeup," said Anna, and they both let out a nervous laugh.

There was a knock at the door, and Rob Shelby cracked it just a bit, asking if he could come in.

"Come in, dear," Anna's mother said.

"Oh, my baby girl," Ron said when he saw his daughter. "You look amazing."

"Thanks, Dad. Please, don't you make me cry, too. I'm already starting to ruin my makeup, and I'm not even anywhere near the altar yet," Anna said.

"I'm sorry dear. You just look so beautiful," he said, then he turned to his wife. "Ellen, they're ready to seat the mother of the bride soon."

"Mother of the bride," Ellen repeated. "Oh, how I've dreamed of this day!" She turned to her daughter and took her hand. "I love you, dear. You just relax and enjoy this day."

"I will, Mom," Anna said.

Her mother reluctantly left the room, and Anna turned to face her father.

"I'm so nervous, Dad," she said.

"You'll be just fine. This is easy. Just a short walk and you're there, getting on with your new life," he said.

"I hope so, Daddy. I love you," she said.

"I love you, too, baby girl," her father said. "And it's time to go."

CHAPTER FIFTY

THE MUSIC WAS PLAYING as Anna and her father started walking out of the room. She knew that Kelly and Rick, arm-in-arm as maid of honor and best man, had already walked almost all the way to the front of the church, and that her cousin's little children, the flower girl and ring bearer, were headed down the aisle now, the little girl dropping rose petals from her basket as she walked slowly forward.

Anna rounded the corner, and the wedding march began to play, and all her friends and family, and Ethan's friends and his family, stood to watch her take slow and careful steps over the carpet of petals.

She saw the smiles on their faces as she passed, but mostly she was looking straight ahead at Ethan, smiling at her from the altar, the pastor just behind him.

Ethan was more handsome than she'd ever seen him, although she didn't know how that was possible. Perhaps it was the glow that radiated from true happiness. He wore a dark grey tuxedo, perfectly tailored. The fine material lay against his muscular frame with a sheen that indicated its fine quality. Even before Anna was very close, she could see the blue of his eyes piercing across the room, gazing at her as if she were the only woman on the planet. And to him, she was.

When Anna and her dad arrived at the front of the church, the music died down and Ron shook Ethan's hand with the smile of a proud father on his face.

Ethan reached out and took Anna's hand.

It was pure bliss, a moment she would remember for the rest of her life, his beautiful eyes looking into hers with the warm glow of true love.

The ceremony seemed to go by quickly, and both Anna and Ethan said the vows they had written without any mistakes. They had rehearsed them so many times they could recite them easily by memory.

And finally, Anna and Ethan heard the words they had both wanted for so long.

"I now pronounce you husband and wife." The pastor smiled warmly. "You may kiss the bride," he added, looking at Ethan.

Ethan put his hand on Anna's cheek and gently caressed her before they both moved in for a passionate kiss. The church exploded with cheers and music played again, and hand-in-hand they walked down the aisle together, shaking hands and hugging their friends and family along the way.

Ethan and Anna stole a few minutes alone in the room where she had gotten dressed earlier. They held each other and kissed, and Anna wiped away her tears of happiness.

"Hello, my wife," he said.

"Hello, my husband," she said back.

Their family and friends had gathered outside, and they all threw rose petals as the couple rushed to their waiting limousine, smiling and waving as they drove off to the reception together.

Most of the town attended either the wedding or the reception, or both, and most thought of Ethan as that handsome and friendly young man who had renovated that old farm out in the country.

But many of them knew the truth, because the entire team from the mansion was also in attendance.

Everyone had a great time at the reception. The couple cut the cake, the wedding party took turns giving toasts to the new couple, and Anna threw her bouquet into a crowd of eager young women.

Kelly caught the bouquet.

She took a victory lap holding the bouquet into the air and ran over to John, throwing her arms around him.

"When do we fly off to Paris for the proposal?" she asked.

"Would you settle for Bluewater?" he laughed, and she rolled her eyes.

"You're a big goof," she said.

Next, it was time for the happy couple's first dance. All eyes turned to Ethan and Anna on the dance floor as the spotlight filtered away everyone else and the lights grew dim. He held her closely and whispered into her ear how much he loved her as they swayed to the soft music.

They looked like they were made for each other, him handsome and muscular, her slender and feminine, both glowing with happiness as they rounded the dance floor, Anna's gown swaying with each step.

Soon it was time for the couple to leave, and all their friends and family waved goodbye as they made their way down the street in their limousine decorated with a "just married" sign.

They spent the night in Ethan's suite in the underground mansion, which they would now share as husband and wife. Ethan had decorated it with flowers, with rose petals sprinkled on the bed and soft music playing. He poured two glasses of champaign.

"A toast to my beautiful bride," he said.

"And to my wonderful, handsome husband," she said.

They made love well into the early morning hours, until the sun broke over the gentle rolling hills of the farmland above them.

* * *

THEY BOARDED THE PRIVATE JET THE NEXT MORNING, STILL EXCITED and awake despite their very late night. They were flying off to their honeymoon, to a resort on a Caribbean Island owned by Ethan and his family.

Anna had no fear this time as the jet took off. Nestled comfortably in her seat next to her husband, she gently spun her wedding ring around and smiled.

They arrived at their destination late in the afternoon and settled into their private suite on the ocean. The view was stunning, with coconut trees swaying in the breeze and bright green tropical plants outlining the bright white sand.

Ethan and Anna ate their first meal of their honeymoon on the veranda overlooking the beach and the crystal-clear ocean, so blue that it almost matched the color of Ethan's eyes.

"I love you so much," he said.

"I love you so much, too," she said.

Later that evening, they took a blanket out to the beach and watched the sun set over the blue ocean waves.

They held each other for hours, looking up at the bright stars in the island sky.

"This is what life is for," said Ethan. "From here, the sky is the limit."

"I can't wait for our future together. How many children do you want?" she asked.

He chuckled. "As many as you want," he said. "There's nothing we can't do together."

Their lips met as they held each other tightly, with the ocean waves gently crashing on the nearby shore and the sounds of crickets singing in the foliage setting the rhythm of nature.

This was contentment. This was the beginning of the rest of their lives. Anna rested her head against Ethan's firm, muscular chest and closed her eyes as she listened to the sound of his heartbeat.

THE END

ALSO BY OLIVIA BHELLE KILDARE

Pregnant With Four Alphas' Babies (writing with Bella Moondragon)

Chosen As the Breeder

Mated to Four Alphas

Threats Against the Breeder

At War for the Breeder

The Stolen Breeder

Four Alphas, Four Babies

Becoming the Luna Queen

Descendants of the Breeder

My Secret Billionaire Series

Finding My Secret Billionaire

Falling for My Secret Billionaire by Bella Moondragon